Dangling

ROBERT WESTHEIMER

ISBN: 154683642X
ISBN 13: 9781546836421

The day was dawning under heavy clouds, portending a storm on the lake. The fishermen, with their nose for the weather, could feel it coming. So they stayed close to shore, huddled in the boat, ready to dash to safety.

After a night of empty nets, the seven men were tired and discouraged. But not just from the fishing. The events of the past week had carried them beyond the limits of their strength. Those events, so unexpected, so confusing and so horrific, had ripped their hearts and minds beyond the breaking point. So they fled to the safety of the familiar, protected by the dark of the night, doing what they knew best.

At the end, only one of them had stood, only one had kept the vigil, had kissed the dead feet of their friend as his body hung lifeless on the shame of the cross. Only one had blood on his face, only one had embraced the mother of their dead friend. The others? Hidden away, cowering in fear.

The loud one, who saw himself as the leader, had to be brought back into the fellowship time and again. He'd already criticized his friend (*"you will <u>never</u> be crucified!"*), denied him (*"I do <u>not know</u> the man"*), and deserted him during the long hours of his friend's painful execution. In his despair, he couldn't possibly know that he would be brought back one more time, and eventually, seal his own fate with a similar execution.

No words were spoken in the calm of the boat. There was none of the earthy grumbling of fishermen who come home empty-handed. A strange numbness enclosed them in a fog, as if the life had been drained from what had once been their livelihood. After the last three years, and especially after the last week, they knew that, familiar as it was, fishing could never restore their spirit.

They would have started for shore sooner, giving up on the fishing, if only there had been something else to do. In their idle moments, they could think only of the terror of the arrest, mock trial and execution. And their own shame. Diversion of any kind was welcome, if ineffective.

Suddenly, a spark of light broke the darkness on the narrow beach. Beside it, a shadowy figure, blurred against the obscurity of the steep shore embankment, turned the spark into a small fire. The mysterious figure seemed to come and go, hidden by the smoke and the lifting night.

The crew watched as the fire grew, and then settled back into glowing coals. Light was beginning to streak the sky, appearing in the cracks between the clouds. In the absence of any other focus, the men were drawn to the fire and to the figure. And after a night of deathly calm, where did this wind suddenly come from?

Then a strangely familiar voice: *"Children, haven't you caught any fish?"*

"No," they answered.

Then a command: *"Cast your nets on the right side, and you will find some!"* Without objection, or any thought of the possible embarrassment if this stranger proved correct, they obeyed.

And there they were, more fish than could be counted, even more than might be safely brought into the boat. Literally right under their noses. How could this mysterious figure have known, standing off in the darkness of the shore?

Suddenly the one who knew him best: *"It is the Lord!"*

The dawn broke, both in the sky and in their hearts. Rays of brilliant light now bathed the beach, clearly showing the profile of a man, standing beside a fire of coals, with food grilling in the rising smoke.

Without a word, the loud one, who saw himself as the leader, impulsively wrapped his tunic around his waist, jumped into the water and swam toward the shore. No words were spoken as the others apprehensively trailed along in the boat, pulling the over-weighted net alongside. Would they be welcomed or would they be chastised by the figure on the beach?

Was it their Lord, who had been brutally killed? This was not his first appearance to them, but perhaps the most unlikely. In ways they could not explain, he seemed the same, yet different.

Drawn to the smell of the breakfast, they heard him direct them to *"bring some of the fish you have just caught."* Later it would occur to them that he often sought and used what they could contribute, giving them a part in his miracles of abundance.

The loud one, Peter, drew the net ashore. They would later count one hundred fifty-three fish, the largest catch any of them ever recalled. Yet the net was intact. And again, they would later remember that the fruit of their missionary work would never tear a net, and that as he had predicted, they would truly become "fishers of men."

"Come and eat breakfast." His words reminded them that his greatest desire was to feed others, not just with food for the body, but with his very self, food for the soul.

And they ate, filling themselves in a way that shed all the gloom of the previous night. The day had truly broken; a new day, a day of reunion with their friend and Lord. They could laugh again.

But Peter's heart still weighed heavily with his failures. And so Jesus, his friend and Lord, sought to reclaim it. They strolled down the beach. Addressing Peter formally, as he had first done three years before, Jesus asked, *"Simon, son of John, do you love me more than these?"*

Seeking to justify himself, Peter responded, *"Yes, Lord, you know that I love you."*

"Then feed my lambs," came the reply.

And once more, Jesus asked Peter if he loved him and again Peter affirmed his love. The third time, Peter was grieved to hear the question repeated and replied *"Lord, you know everything; you know that I love you."*

"Feed my sheep," the answer came again.

And then: *"Truly I tell you, when you were young, you dressed yourself and walked where you wanted to. But when you are old, you will stretch out your hands, and another will dress you and take you where you do not wish to go."*

And so, Simon son of John, the critic and denier of Jesus, was restored to Peter, the Rock. But with an accompanying promise of future suffering. This time, Peter made no comment; he did not question or deny his Lord's ominous prophecy. Perhaps by now, he'd learned to keep quiet and just accept the words of Jesus. So instead, he changed the subject.

Turning, he saw another, trailing behind them. This was the other disciple, the one who had faithfully stood at Golgotha, who Jesus had entrusted with his mother, the one who seemed closest to Jesus, the beloved disciple, the "one whom Jesus loved." Without even mentioning his name, Peter asked, *"What about this man?"*

The response to Peter's pointed question has puzzled the faithful through the ages, a prophecy that could not be understood or believed in any literal sense.

"If he is to remain until I come again, what is that to you?"

And Peter was again, speechless.

(From the Gospel of John, chapter 21.)

1

Millie was born under a promise. It wasn't one of those stunning prophecies that knocks everyone to the ground within two miles of hearing it. Nor was it one of those eerie promises that can't be understood until you read Nostradamus' sixteenth quatrain while standing on your head. No, this was a promise, a prophecy really, that would have been forgotten except for who delivered it, and for the few who remembered it.

Millie's promise came from her Uncle Evan, who appeared out of nowhere at Millie's baptism ceremony. To the relief of the family, Uncle Evan had not been seen in recent times. Certain members of the family were sure that he lived under a bridge with his favorite companion, a bottle of cheap whiskey. That, of course, is why he was not invited to the baptism.

But there Evan was, full of himself (and probably more), standing by the priest at the ceremony like he was one of the inner circle. Some of those present wondered if he was simply paying his dues to appear later at the reception, at which alcohol would be served.

So what was Uncle Evan's promise? It should have been yesterday's news, and would have been quickly forgotten if it hadn't been so doggone clever.

Standing in a circle around the baptismal fountain, with the priest solemnly explaining why it was a good thing to anoint Millie's infant head with oil, Uncle Evan swayed a bit as he stood. Unexpectedly, he spoke, emitting a prophecy (together with a good deal of fumes) that was forever remembered by at least one of those present.

"Why, this baby is not who she seems to be," Evan proclaimed, temporarily forgetting Millie's name. "She has a hidden quality that will not show up for decades. She's the dangling thread that when you pull it, it simply gets longer and longer until you reach something quite unexpected."

The infant Millie was, of course, oblivious to Uncle Evan's promise. And Evan, who re-submerged soon after the baptism, never explained what he meant, mostly because no one ever asked him. If it hadn't been for the priest, Father Vlacek, Millie would never have heard the story. But Father heard. From then on, Father called Millie his "dangling thread."

Now, almost fifty years later, Uncle Evan was most certainly gone, taking his secrets with him. Father was gone too. He now occupied an honored place in the graveyard by the little church at Plostina, under the spreading branches of the live oak tree that as a young priest, he had planted decades before.

And among Millie's most prized possessions was a gift, a life marker that mysteriously arrived not long after her baptism: a smooth wooden box containing a linen handkerchief with a single thread dangling from one corner. Millie's mother kept the box until her first communion, giving it to her with a brief explanation about how special she was, especially to Father Vlacek. Uncle Evan, the donor of the gift, was omitted from the redacted story.

Without knowing the history of the box or the thread, Millie knew that she and this gift were connected in some way. Her only memory was Father's familiar nickname: "Millie, you're just a dangling thread."

He'd go on: *"There's more to you than anyone knows. And some day, someone will pull that thread. And when that happens, we will all find out how special you really are."*

■ ■ ■

We live in a dangerous time. Physical security and the protection of leaders are at a premium. Abraham Lincoln received ordinary citizens at the

White House and walked the streets of Washington, D.C. Today, our leaders, and even our self-styled celebrities are surrounded by layers of protection, both physical and digital, as if inside a steel cocoon. We can never return to that quieter day when safety (and harmony) could be assumed.

Millie had grown up at the end of that safer time, the fifties, when parents' chief fears for their children were (1) polio and (2) becoming trapped in an abandoned refrigerator. Millie never contracted polio and to be honest, she never even saw an abandoned refrigerator. But continuously reminded by her parents, she diligently kept a sharp lookout for one.

Millie's home town of Plostina was a small village in the rolling hills of central Texas. Settled in the nineteenth century by Czech immigrants fleeing the Old World for a better life, it retained much of the spiritual and agricultural heritage of its pioneer forebears. Most of the current families could trace back to those ancestral roots, and their food, language and values were as unchanged as possible in this new dangerous and digital age.

As she grew, Millie felt increasingly led to leave the quiet and safety of Plostina for the larger world. While she wasn't sure exactly where her life would lead her, she knew that she would not stay forever in Plostina.

Leaving for the big university in Austin seemed to Millie like entering a new world, one that opened too many doors, offered too many paths and one that seemed complex beyond her capacity. Her personality had been formed in a quieter life, one that she was surprised to learn was outside the mainstream. But always, there was the dangling thread, a promise of something beyond her reach, a life that she could not fathom, an adventure without a road map. Perhaps a college education was a first step toward that life.

If the dangling thread was ever to be pulled to its full length, it would have to be by someone (or something) else. Millie could never pull it by herself. As much as she could, she stayed in a bubble of her own creation, living what she thought was a low-risk existence, prepared for a predictable, if not exciting, future. That worked … for a while.

Time passed. Now in her forties, Millie had made an uneasy peace with this dangerous time. Comfortable or not, she'd been led into the mainstream. The Old World values of her family were buried somewhere deep in her personality, dormant, but not dead. Her lifestyle was now urban, with Plostina left far behind in that hilltop cemetery alongside her parents, grandparents and Father. She carefully guarded her two children, Paul and Leslie, as they grew through childhood, not in the tranquility of Plostina, but in suburban Houston, with school populations in the thousands and inside a melting pot of nationalities, languages and beliefs. There was no Father Vlacek, no figure of stability and faith.

And yet below her self-controlled surface was a flowing current, a calling that she could not name and would not publicly acknowledge. Eventually, there would be something more to her life, something out there, drawing her to an undefined future. Deep down, the dangling thread was alive, waiting for someone or something to pull it with a force that would take it all the way to a deeper place, wilder and more unpredictable than she'd ever known. It was easy to suppress for a time, as the early years of marriage and motherhood consumed her attention. But that restless feeling would not go away and it increasingly resonated below the surface, even as her will tried to suppress it from above.

Randall, Millie's husband, was born of the city. He was attracted to her simplicity, and he might even say her innocence and naiveté. At heart, she was everything she seemed to be: she lacked the ambition to pretend to be any more than who she was on the inside. With her natural manner and ease at conversation, Millie complemented his cerebral awkwardness. People easily accepted Millie, even when she spoke honest criticism. There was no subtext to her, no reason to wonder what she really thought.

Randall, on the other hand, was a thinker. His calculating words frequently seemed to veil hidden motives and a personal agenda.

Compared to Millie, Randall was seemingly more complex. Had you peeled him like an onion, you'd have discovered a core that wasn't too different from hers. But unlike Millie, Randall had created layers of images, working definitions of himself that he employed to navigate the different stages upon which his life was acted out.

He was the consummate professional at work, the friendly but not-too-approachable neighbor, and the upright, totally respectable parishioner at church. Also the faithful, if not passionate, husband. All of his personas had to be precisely juggled so that he presented just the right Randall for every possible circumstance, custom-tailored for each audience.

Millie had been attracted to his sophistication, to his ability to think his way through complex life situations, to take work and social relationships only far enough to keep them from exposing any more of himself than he wished to give them. He would not allow anyone to encroach too deeply into his inner thoughts and feelings.

She, on the other hand, was like a children's storybook, spontaneously exploring life with innocence and aplomb; but he was a mystery novel, waiting and contemplating before attempting to say or do the perfect thing. For him, life played out at arms-length, needing to be studied before he could compose a course of action that best served him.

Randall's lifestyle compromises dug not nearly so deeply as hers. Comfortable with trading off childhood values for the adult values of twenty-first century corporate America, he navigated life on a path of ambition, focusing more on life goals than on life values. His core of integrity eroded away, a bit at a time, all in the cause of achieving success. This surgery of values happened so cleanly that he never felt even a pang or a twinge.

Millie, on the other hand, keenly felt the pain of loss, a sort of grieving for her compromises. She regretted that her children did not have a nearby extended family, as she'd enjoyed as a child. There was no Father Vlacek, no grandparents, and no generational pipeline of values that could be traced back to the old country and to pioneer ancestors. Her ties to the past had been broken and could not be mended under the sea of middle class roofs that Millie now called home. She grieved over these losses.

She thought of herself as a not-too-good wife and mother, significantly underestimating both the challenges she faced and her ability to face them. Randall, on the other hand, in every decision, every conversation, every family project, had to be right. All of the time. He took the role of the intellectual alpha figure in the household, thereby shoving Millie into a deep second place, almost a second-class family citizenship. He was the strategist and leader, while she was the one who cleaned the toilets.

As a result, their marriage followed a course of increasing distance; polite, but playing out at a mostly surface level. The chill crept in almost unnoticed. They knew their respective roles and over the years, they became adept at the dance of playing at marriage, functioning more like roommates than deeply engaged spouses. Neither could put their finger on this. It happened so gradually, but both could sense the erosion into a life of married singles, playing out each day following an unwritten script aimed at nothing more than keeping the peace. For the most part, it seemed to work.

In college, Millie had majored in archeology. Her parents thought it frivolous. But she had a genuine affinity for antiquity, for analyzing the past in great detail to explain the life patterns of long ago. Her favorite was ancient Egypt, with its hieroglyphic writings and massive monuments. There, examining ancient artifacts preserved in the dry air of the desert, she could see antiquity as if it had been produced yesterday.

In an amateurish way, she kept up with this interest during the early years of her marriage. Before Paul was born, she had worked at the museum of natural history. Her clerical job was not, in fact, professional archeology, but it did keep her close enough to sustain the modest flame of this interest.

And what about the dangling thread? Life had tugged a bit on the thread, though not so hard as to pull it completely. Millie dutifully tried to lead what she thought was a normal life, one that avoided any call to adventure. She simply let her days play out within a set of narrow, self-imposed boundaries, living on a predictable path of least resistance. But in her deeper thoughts, Millie wondered if someday, the thread might be pulled. She still remembered the smooth wooden box. It remained hidden in a drawer, and Millie assumed that its promise for her life would remain hidden as well. As she was about to learn, however, Millie was wrong.

2

It was an otherwise ordinary day, but the phone call turned out to be anything but ordinary. The caller was Professor Chandler, Millie's mentor from college.

Eugene Chandler held the position of Professor Emeritus of Archeology. He'd been recently tenured two decades before, when Millie took his classes at the university. Now semi-retired and widowed, he taught part-time on campus. In his private hours, he tended the garden on his hilltop home outside of Austin. Millie had been one of Chandler's early favorites. She'd worked part-time in his office, grading papers and running errands for him. To reward her, he'd allowed her to intern for him even before she graduated. The highlight of her internship was a dig in Egypt, a memory she still treasured.

Now, twenty years later, Dr. Chandler was clearly aging. Millie phoned him once a month, just to keep up, and visited him whenever she was in Austin. She had attended the memorial service for Clara, his wife of fifty-two years, and Millie's presence was a great consolation to him. It had become increasingly clear to her that his own health was now declining and that, childless, he had virtually no family support. So she felt pleased to periodically reach out to him, and doubly pleased to hear from him when he called.

"Millie," he exclaimed in his excited, high-pitched voice, "I have a new project for you!" She was amused that his greeting sounded so much like the professor from her past, giving her yet another class assignment.

"I've been contacted by some researchers who need help with a project that you will find very interesting. And it could give us a chance to work together again. Are you listening?"

"Yes, Dr. Chandler, I'm listening, but you must know that my archeological skills are rusty beyond repair. I'd love to work with you again but I don't want to disappoint you. Remember, it's been decades since I was your student."

The momentary silence from his end told Millie that her less-than-eager response had surprised him. She knew that he remembered her as a young, energetic student, one who would say yes to anything he proposed. But of course, by now, she was a middle-aged wife and mother. She had responsibilities.

He pressed ahead anyway: "Millie, I want you for this project. And it's not really archeology, anyway. A team has been formed and they want an archeologist to be involved. I'm not actually on the team but will be available for consultation if needed."

"Dr. Chandler, I'm a bit confused. What is this all about?" His invitation both surprised and pleased her, but she still felt in the dark.

"Sorry to be so mysterious. Let me explain. A foundation, which shall remain nameless, has funded research to prove or disprove a theory related to ancient writings. They have hired a director who is building a team of researchers to carry out the project. I've been engaged to help put the team together and oversee the project. I want you on the team. So what do you say?"

She could hear the excitement in his faltering voice and wanted to say yes to Dr. Chandler's obscure proposal. But even more than her age, motherhood and marital woes, Millie had a problem: she'd suffered a disability some years after college, one that she'd never shared with Dr. Chandler. To her, this disability was potentially serious enough to prevent her from accepting his invitation. She'd need to know more.

"Dr. Chandler, you know that I love you and want to help. I really do. Honest. But you still haven't explained what this is all about."

"Oh, I haven't?"

"No, Dr. Chandler, you haven't."

"Well, let me begin again, from the beginning. Of course. I should explain." And Dr. Chandler began again:

"Millie, are you aware of the emerging field of the scientific study of writings? You may remember a few years ago, an anonymous author penned an infamous book about a certain political figure. No one knew who wrote the book, and it became a sort of national detective game to identify this mysterious author. Using sophisticated computer programs that could read and analyze mountains of text in seconds, an answer was found. The suspected author, a university professor, finally admitted that he wrote the book.

"This science, called stylometry, goes back centuries. For example, the letters of the Apostle Paul have been studied for word usage, sentence structure and so on, and it has been found that these letters were actually written by multiple authors. Of course, that doesn't mean that Paul didn't authorize them or even in some ways dictate them, though not necessarily word for word. But in any case, this science is becoming more prevalent in certain university settings. It can also be used forensically to determine authorship in legal matters.

"So now, Millie, do you see what this is all about?" He paused for her answer.

Frustrated, she responded, "No, Dr. Chandler, I don't. I need to know more. What is the theory that we will analyze and why is it so important? And how could it possibly involve ancient writings?"

"You see, Millie," he went on, "the powerful computer programs now used in stylometry have only recently been upgraded to enable them to cross over between multiple languages. Do you know what that means?"

Without pausing, he answered his own question: "Millie, it means that it's now possible to analyze writings across languages and even across long distances of time. So we can look at ancient writings, for example, in Greek, and compare them stylistically to modern English texts."

"But Dr. Chandler," she was getting more confused, "why would any-one want to analyze ancient writings to compare to contemporary authors?

Ancient and modern texts couldn't possibly match. There's no way that they could have the same authors."

"Yes, of course, that is what you might assume," Dr. Chandler went on. "But not so fast, Millie, not so fast! You see, one of the graduate students on the team testing the new software was playing around with it one day. He decided to see what might happen when texts from different languages and eras were compared. By pure chance, he selected a Biblical text, the Gospel of John, which was written in Greek in the first century. To his surprise, the Gospel of John produced several 'hits' when compared across centuries and languages."

"What do you mean 'hits?'"

"It all happened by accident, you see, all by accident. He entered the Gospel of John and the system scanned the database for texts that might match in style, vocabulary, sentence structure and so on, that could have been written by the same author. Not only did the system find several possible matches, it found them in different countries, using different languages and hundreds of years apart!"

"But Dr. Chandler," she was struggling to put her mind around what she had just heard, "how can that be possible? The author of the Gospel of John was one of Jesus' early disciples, the Apostle John. So he couldn't possibly have lived beyond the first century. It just couldn't be the same person. That's impossible!"

"Yes of course, Millie, you are correct. Of course! It's impossible! But don't you see, that is exactly what we need to find out. How *could* it be possible? Could texts written hundreds of years apart in different languages actually have been written by the same person? You have hit the nail on the head and that's why I want you on this project."

"Do you mean, Dr. Chandler," she said carefully, "that you want me and some others to determine if the Apostle John could be living all these centuries later, and might still be alive and actively writing today? Dr. Chandler, are you serious?"

"Yes, Millie, I am dead serious. Dead serious. And you are right, Millie, that's exactly what I'm inviting you to do. But that's not all. We don't just want to find out if it's actually possible. This isn't just an academic exercise to prove a theory. The theory will be nothing more than a theory unless …."

"Unless what, Dr. Chandler? It seems to me that even if we do prove the theory that the Apostle John *could* somehow be alive today and actively writing, that no one will ever believe us!"

"Yes, Millie, you are exactly right! Precisely! No one will believe it. The theory that the Apostle John could be the author of all these texts and is still alive and active today will be nothing more than a theory unless … unless you actually find him, and bring him out of hiding for all the world to see."

3

The thought of Dr. Chandler's project both intrigued and frightened Millie. Could she do this? She wasn't exactly sure what would be asked of her. And she still had trouble believing that Dr. Chandler's theory about the Apostle John might be true. It sounded completely impossible. She would need more information, of course. But if the project required any strenuous physical activity, she would need to decline.

Millie had never told Dr. Chandler about the lingering disability from her past. Her role was to support him in his senior years, and she didn't want him to worry about her, especially about her disability. While she could hide it from him during her brief visits to Austin, in her own mind, Millie thought of herself as damaged, unable to respond to any physical demands beyond the most basic.

Three years before, Millie had awakened one day to a strange feeling of weakness in her hands and feet. Walking became awkward and daily tasks like opening jars and tying her shoes suddenly seemed difficult. She brushed this off at first, deciding that it would go away on its own. She thought to herself, *I can't be sick; I'm too busy to be sick!*

The weakness grew worse over the next two days, progressing up her arms and legs. Now, she was unsteady on her feet. Simple acts like opening drawers became almost impossible. At times, she felt a tingling sensation in her arms and legs.

On the third day, she told Randall that she needed to see a doctor. The weakness was growing, and she was afraid to drive. Randall left work to take Millie to see Dr. Miller, their primary care physician, who immediately admitted her to the hospital.

After a day of tests, Millie's weakness was progressing toward her interior muscular system, and her breathing was becoming labored. She felt no pain with this mysterious condition, but the weakness and tingling feeling continued to worsen.

The tests confirmed what Dr. Miller had suspected: "Millie, you're suffering from Guillain-Barre Syndrome (pronounced "Geeyon Baray"), a neurological condition resulting in muscular weakness, and in its advanced stage, paralysis. There is no known cause and no known cure. Most patients experience a slow reversal of the effects, though many suffer lingering weakness for the rest of their lives."

He went on: "Severe cases of Guillain-Barre require a respirator, as the muscles controlling breathing are effectively shut down by the disease. Without a respirator, these patients can literally die from suffocation. Fortunately, Millie, your case is a moderate one, and a respirator is not needed."

After three days in the hospital, it became clear that the disease had run its course and she could be released.

However, Millie's extremities were now too weak for her to function normally. For a month, she was wheel-chair bound and essentially helpless. A full-time caregiver was required to assist her with even the most basic of activities.

Then, she graduated to a walker and finally, a full year of braces on her legs. Even afterwards, she was forced to resort to the braces at the end of a tiring day. Her hands shook, and she could not control them as before. Simple tasks such as handwriting and fastening a button remained difficult. Overall, her coordination would never be the same.

Millie was struck with this mysterious illness just as she had begun to serve as a cheerleader mom for Leslie's high school pep squad. She was forced to give it up, struggling to explain what had happened to both of her disappointed children. She was unable to cook

Thanksgiving dinner, and lacked the strength and dexterity to wrap Christmas presents that year.

All of this served to shake Millie's confidence. It reinforced not only her mortality, but also her sense of fitness for whatever the future might hold. The weakness she now experienced slowed her down, requiring her to consider each task in light of these new physical limitations. It was clear that she could no longer perform to the standard that she'd set for herself. Each physical act was now compromised in a way that she had never imagined. She would never again feel whole.

Such was the "new normal" that Millie faced. After a year, her condition stabilized into a murky weakness. Navigating her world felt like an existence under water, attempting to live in the face of a permanently-strong current. When she tired, the symptoms returned, almost as strong as at first.

As she contemplated the future, all Millie could see was a life damaged by this infirmity. Any thought of the dangling thread, and its promise of a higher calling to her life, seemed destined to be an unfulfilled prophecy. There would be no "flowing current" of great potential for Millie. Father Vlacek must have been wrong.

And now, at middle age, and in the wake of the unusual invitation from Dr. Chandler, Millie was torn. To her surprise, the research project that he offered struck a chord deep inside her, even if it had all been quite vague. And in a strange way, the vagueness actually appealed to her sense of adventure, which had lain dormant all through the early years of her marriage and motherhood.

After several days of troubled self-examination, Millie packed a bag and headed for the Abbey of St. Therese. Operated by Carmelite sisters, the abbey would be a place of refuge, a harbor where she could feel safe and contemplate Dr. Chandler's offer. Millie wasn't quite sure what to hope for, but she felt confident that she would find peace at the abbey.

As she packed her things, her hand ran across the smooth wooden box from her infancy, the one containing the linen cloth with the dangling thread. Without opening it, Millie placed the box in her bag and walked out the door. She left Randall a note telling him where she was going, but omitting any explanation.

Millie's time at the Abbey did not produce lightning bolts of inspiration. The Abbey's ministry is one of solitude, and guests are expected to remain silent, unless speaking with one of the spiritual directors. Millie did visit several times with one of them, Sister Camilla. And although the visits were pleasant, they were nothing more than that. The time spent in silence, however, was, surprisingly, quite restorative to her.

One comment from Sister Camilla, however, stuck with Millie and she allowed it to return to her thoughts as she drove home from the Abbey.

"Millie," Sister observed, "your distress puts you in good company: you should know that people of faith are not exempt from suffering and from feeling out of control. Over the centuries of our faith, those we revere the most have suffered in some way, or lived with incredible uncertainty. When we experience pain, and when we face an uncertain future, we are mystically linked to the suffering of Christ, and to the very pain of God. I urge you, Millie, to let this play out and see what God will do with it. You can experience life with all its failures and suffering without judging yourself inadequate. Eventually, you will see God's hand in your distress."

While at the Abbey, Millie did not use her phone or check messages. Upon returning home, she noticed several voice mails from Dr. Chandler. One in particular seemed to speak to the depth of her conflicted feelings:

"Millie," the high-pitched voice began, "I hope that you are still considering my invitation to join our project. You know how highly I regard you, Millie. I'm sure you know that. But it's more, and I can't adequately put into words the feeling that you are truly called to do this. I don't mean so much that you should say yes because the project needs you so badly, or because I would enjoy your company so much. It's more than that: I have this feeling that you need to do this for *you*, for your own sake. Maybe that doesn't make sense and you must excuse the ramblings of an old man.

"Millie, I have been a scientist all of my life but now, in my old age, I rely so much more on my feelings. And my feeling about you is so strong, that you need to do this project. Yes, that's right. That's right, Millie, so strong. So please, Millie, call me back and let me know."

Millie played this message again and again. But she could not yet bring herself to return his call.

Finally, after several indecisive days, she phoned Dr. Chandler.

"Dr. Chandler, I just need more time to consider your offer and your project. Is that all right? I mean, don't you want me to be absolutely sure about this? I feel so torn. Could you give me two weeks to think about it?

"Of course, Millie," he responded. "Anyway, the foundation is still working to finalize the project's funding, so I don't need an immediate answer. We can wait a while.

"But Millie," he went on, "you may never be totally sure about this. I realize it's something out of the blue and that you were not looking for this project. In my experience, Millie, there are very few absolutes in life. And if you wait to be absolutely sure, you may never experience life to its fullest.

"But yes, Millie, take some more time to think it over."

Over the next weeks, Millie grew more faithful in her spiritual disciplines. For some unknown reason, her prayer life began to come alive, with a feeling of being filled as she prayed, often in complete silence. Her prayers were no longer one-way appeals; the periods of silence were remarkably filled in a way that she could not explain. She began to read scripture, following a *lectio divina* style, a few verses a day. And the familiar words of the gospels seemed to take on a life of their own and truly speak to her. At times, the text seemed to just jump off the page. She started a journal, capturing what the words of scripture spoke to her.

However, none of this produced an answer to Dr. Chandler's invitation. Internally, though, she was feeling uplifted, and she felt a peace that she hadn't before. In a way beyond any known logic, she was being fed by a spirit that seemed to come from the inside.

The two weeks passed.

As she went through the pros and cons, Millie considered her marriage and her children. Randall knew nothing of Dr. Chandler's invitation. If she accepted, there would be an unpleasant confrontation. Randall would cross-examine her, probing for any weakness in her story. He would attempt to prove to her that she was making a foolish mistake.

Paul was now a senior in college and Leslie had recently left for her freshman year. Their lives would experience no disruption if Millie accepted Dr. Chandler's invitation. Millie had to admit that with a marriage that was just going through the motions, together with this loss of her purpose as a mother, her loneliness had now become acute.

The bigger concern in her mind was what Millie considered to be her disability. She had not told Dr. Chandler about it, and would not do so, no matter what. She wanted him to think of her, and to remember her the way she was, whole and without any infirmity. But she knew that she couldn't put him off any longer. He needed an answer.

As she reflected on the phone conversations with Dr. Chandler, it occurred to Millie that she could not rationalize or logically justify getting involved. *What could I bring to such a project anyway?* There were too many unanswered questions, too much uncertainty. And she was too scarred by her physical disability and by a disappointing marriage. She would have to gracefully turn him down.

Millie prayed for direction. She scanned scripture, searching for a clue. Hoping for an answer, she got none. After several days of wrestling with it, she got out of bed on a Saturday morning, had her coffee and phoned Dr. Chandler.

"Dr. Chandler," she began and before she could go on, he interrupted.

"Millie I am so glad you phoned. I've been thinking of nothing but you for the past week, hoping you'd call me back. You know, I am quite fond of you. Now what do you have to tell me?"

"Dr. Chandler, you know that I'm fond of you, too," she responded, haltingly. "And I've thought a lot about your project and about your invitation. But I just have to say that ... against my better judgment, I am going to go out on a big limb ... and accept your invitation to join your project."

The words were out of Millie's mouth before her brain could stop them. And in the moment, her thoughts flashed back to another person who she knew loved her, Father Vlacek, whose words of long ago suddenly resurfaced:

> *"There's more to you than anyone knows. And some day, someone will pull that thread. And when that happens, we will all find out how special you really are."*

Those words had not crossed her mind for years. In truth, Millie had given up on the wooden box containing the linen cloth with the dangling thread. But now, in this moment, when exciting new possibilities clashed with years of discouragement, a flicker of hope began to burn inside of her. She *could* do this! Whatever might be involved, she *could* do it and if it demanded more of her than she could give, then strength from outside of her would have to carry her through.

4

"You're going to *what?*" was Randall's reaction when Millie told him that she'd agreed to join Dr. Chandler's project. "Let me get this straight. You are going on a hunt for someone who's been dead for almost two thousand years? Sure, that makes all the sense in the world. When you find him, don't forget to say hello to his friends, Aristotle and Confucius. They probably live in the same apartment complex or work out at the same gym.

"Millie, you've gone off your rocker. And your loyalty to that dementia-ridden professor is pathetic! If you really want to find the Apostle John, if he ever even really existed, you're going to have to take along a pretty strong shovel!"

The more he put her down, the stronger became her resolve. In a way that she thought probably perverse, his opposition was exactly what she needed. She smiled to herself with an inner satisfaction, careful not to egg him on too much with an open display of pleasure at his ranting.

When he demanded details, she of course, could not provide them. She'd accepted purely on trust and on the feeling that this was a calling that she could not refuse. Millie had never been one for adventure, but now, in her forties, it was time to take the plunge. She could not imagine that this project might actually involve any kind of danger.

Millie observed that Randall stopped short of threatening any action against her for what he termed her "middle-aged lunacy." She could not know that the skeletons in his own closet were keeping him from attacking her too far.

His final challenge was "Millie, why on earth are you doing this?" In light of his prowess at arguing, this question seemed juvenile to her, but in an unvarnished way, it drove to the heart of the matter.

She thought her response, "I don't really know, Randall, I just feel called to do it," would provoke another tirade, but it did not. The conversation was over.

■ ■ ■

An orientation meeting was held to introduce all of the project team members. The team leader, a representative of the anonymous foundation, conducted the meeting, with help from Dr. Chandler.

Dressed in a navy blue suit, white shirt and red tie, the team leader, Douglas Parks, looked the part of corporate America. He was all business, producing an agenda, a Powerpoint presentation, and polite but very brief introductions of the team members. There was no ice-breaker exercise and it became immediately clear to Millie that the term "team" was meant in only the most nominal sense. There was no explanation as to why the unnamed foundation was interested in the project and it was also clear that neither Dr. Chandler nor any of the four other members had initiated it. But this was undoubtedly a significant priority to someone, somewhere in the mysterious foundation. No additional background was given.

The other odd thing was confidentiality.

Parks explained, "There is to be no coverage of this project, and all findings are to be tightly kept within the team. Each team member will sign a non-disclosure agreement, indicating that you will communicate nothing of this project to any outside party. That includes family, friends, anyone and everyone."

The secrecy was a bit unnerving to Millie, who imagined that the world should hear if the theory about John was correct.

The graduate student who'd stumbled onto the analysis of the Gospel of John was present to explain his process and how it all came about. His name was Khurum and his accent made understanding him quite difficult. All that Millie could determine was that the software's database was quite massive, reaching across many computer servers, and that the analysis could take any written material of suitable length and seek matches in terms of vocabulary, style, sentence structure, etc. It was not a perfect system, especially when crossing over the barriers of multiple languages.

However, with a high degree of statistical probability, the Gospel of John had matched about twenty documents, ranging from a third century gospel that was excluded from the canon, to a twelfth century manuscript from a Greek Orthodox monk, and on into more modern writings. Languages included Greek, Latin, Old High German, Shakespearean English, Spanish, modern French, and modern English. Most of the writings were no more than ten pages in length, and all shared a highly spiritual theme. The authors of most of them had been tentatively identified, though the more ancient ones needed further review. Khurum added, to Millie's surprise, that processing was ongoing and that it was likely that even more matches would be found.

In addition to the involvement of Dr. Chandler, the team had access to experts who could assist with the more obscure languages.

A representative of the Vatican, Monsignor Francis Morelli, was a member of the team. He would provide access to the archives of the Vatican in case more matches were found, and in case the trail led to clerics of the church.

The other team members included two representatives from the Dutch technology company that had developed the software: Hans Oltorf, who was a marketing executive, and Marianne Weems, a programmer who had written much of the program code. In addition, the team included Hugh Matthews, a Cambridge English professor of Shakespearean literature and an expert on medieval writings. All except Millie had some experience with stylometry, computer programming, ancient languages, or the church. Compared to the others, her lack of credentials was an unspoken question, at least in her mind. It wouldn't be the last time she wondered why she'd been picked for the project.

Each team member received a briefing book.

"You are to keep this book in the strictest confidence and show it to no one, not even to family members," Parks instructed. "There will be no electronic versions of anything, and no communication via email or texting."

The book contained a biography of the Apostle John, together with some of the ancient and contemporary writings that had matched his gospel. The names of the presumed authors of these writings were not included.

Parks quickly summarized the biography.

"The Apostle John," he began, "was one of the twelve, the closest disciples of Jesus. He and his older brother James were fishermen, and were among the first disciples called by Jesus. His gospel, one of four in the New Testament, is known for its poetic writings and for its deep theology. Unlike the other gospels, John goes into themes of love, light and truth. He is the only gospel writer to record Jesus' washing the feet of the others during the Last Supper, and he was the only disciple to witness the crucifixion of Jesus. From the cross, Jesus asked John to care for his mother, Mary. John was known as the "disciple whom Jesus loved." He can be seen in Leonardo DaVinci's "Last Supper" sitting next to Jesus. In addition to his gospel, John also wrote several letters that are in the New Testament, and some believe that he also wrote the book of Revelation, the last book of the Bible."

Next, Parks reviewed the methodology for the team. It would involve personal visits to the candidates who had been identified by the software. The personal visits would aim at encouraging the Apostle John to reveal himself, avoiding any direct questions about identity. It would be unlikely for the Apostle John to reveal himself in the first meeting – it would take time to expect him to open up and admit who he was. As a result, multiple visits to promising candidates would likely be required. The teams were warned not to attempt to move the conversation along too quickly, for fear of driving the candidate deep underground.

Secrecy was critically important. *How many more times will we hear that?* she wondered, especially as the candidates were approached. Each team must have a cover, or announced reason for the visit that would not raise suspicion as to their true purpose.

"It should be assumed," Parks went on, "that John will not wish to be found and that he will be adept at hiding. Otherwise, he would have already revealed himself over the centuries, and not written using so many other names. No assumptions should be made about his appearance, ethnicity, language, education, vocation, age or even gender. He could literally be anyone, anywhere."

Parks did not allow questions from the team. Millie had several that she would have liked to ask.

First, it was not clear to her why there were multiple matches within the same time period. Even going back to manuscripts from the middle-ages, writings of the same period -- originating in different countries and even in different languages -- matched the Gospel of John in style and content. Likewise, contemporary writings had surfaced in England, France and Guatemala. Clearly, the Apostle John could not be in three places at the same time.

Millie wondered if that meant that the software was flawed. All would need to be researched.

Dr. Chandler intercepted Millie as she left the meeting. "How do you think it went?" She knew that he'd want her to be pleased and committed. But she had to be honest with him.

"I'm not sure, Dr. Chandler. I felt so out of place and couldn't help wondering why I was there."

He replied, "By the time this is over, Millie, I promise you will know."

A week later, she was given her first assignment. Millie was to investigate the Guatemalan source, an individual named Victor Cardenas, a parish priest living in the outskirts of Antigua. Her briefing materials included several of his writings that had matched in the computer database to first century writings of John the Apostle. The longest of these, a letter written to the Vatican supporting the poor in Guatemala, had been circulated in the US and was widely known for its passionate appeal for the peasant class.

Millie hurriedly prepared, obtaining her passport, touching base with Paul and Leslie to make sure that they were all right before she left. They, of course, could not be told the real reason why Millie was making this trip, so she claimed to be going to a Spanish immersion class.

Everything was moving at a rapid pace and Millie didn't have time to fully weigh the risks and challenges that she might face. She packed her braces and hoped that she would not need them.

Millie's tickets arrived by private courier, together with hotel reservations and information on transportation. She would be met by a driver at the Guatemala City airport. No name was given.

Then, two days before she was to leave for Guatemala, Millie's phone rang. On the other end was a neighbor, with news of Randall.

"Millie," she began, "I wanted to let you know that this morning, I saw Randall and a woman who appeared to be a female co-worker at the airport, walking to a car in the parking garage. They looked quite chummy."

"Oh yes," Millie assured her, "I know all about that. You see, Randall has been out of town on business, and was due back this morning. And I also knew that he was traveling with the woman you saw, who is one of his long-time business associates. I've known her and her husband for years and I'm sure that she was the one you saw."

But in truth, Millie had not known who was with Randall. And worse, Randall wasn't expected home until the following day. He'd evidently come home a day early. Millie spent that night wondering where he was and who he was with.

"Tell me about your trip," Millie inquired when Randall came home the following evening.

"Nothing special, just a series of meetings and nothing much accomplished," came the reply. "Business as usual."

"Were you traveling with anyone?"

"Yes, several people were on this trip, including Max from Sales and Gretchen from HR. We've all traveled together before. Why do you ask?"

Millie did not pursue this further. Had her physical disability played a part in this? Had Randall cooled toward her because of her damaged state? Millie was shaken down to her core. To Millie, faithfulness in marriage was taken for granted, an absolute not to be violated. Pursuing the matter was not only a sign of failure, it was a marker of a marriage that had been gradually deteriorating for years. Even so, her pain at this revelation was worse than anything she'd ever felt.

While she had no choice but to acknowledge it, Millie would live with this new setback, as long as it got no worse and as long as it stayed hidden. Protecting her children from this turn in her marriage became Millie's priority. She would not expose them to Randall's infidelities. She would tough it out. In the moment, she even thought that perhaps it was all her fault anyway.

As she looked back over her adult life, Millie viewed little more than one loss after another. First, she had lost the support systems of her childhood and youth. For a time, she filled the void as her family consumed her energy and attention.

But now, after learning to live with the loss of her physical health and after suffering the pain of an unfaithful husband, the family dynamic had changed. Perhaps this new calling had come at just the right time, serving to open a new chapter in Millie's life. She could only wonder. For now, she was committed to Dr. Chandler's project and to finding Father Victor Cardenas in Antigua, Guatemala.

Settling into her seat on the plane, Millie was surprised to look up and see Marianne Weems boarding and sitting down next to Millie. She'd not been told about her travel companion, though Marianne seemed not the least puzzled.

Their in-flight conversation was strained, as neither knew what the other had been told about their assignment. And of course, both had been introduced at the briefing meeting in only the most surface manner. Marianne, Millie remembered, was one of the developers of the software used in the analysis. She understood from the briefing that the matches were useful only so far, in narrowing the field of candidates. Personal interviews, such as the one they were assigned to, would be necessary to authoritatively confirm the identity of John.

As they landed in the dark in Guatemala City, Millie observed that the runways were ringed by what appeared to be black snow. It was, in fact, ash from a recent small eruption from one of the surrounding volcanoes.

She was surprised to learn that Central Guatemala is filled with both active and dormant volcanoes. Although there had not been a major eruption for years, small ones frequently deposit layers of fine ash across the area.

Overall, the gloomy piles of the dark ash, together with the strained conversation with Marianne, served to chill Millie's attitude to this first assignment. She had no idea of what lay ahead.

5

Once they had landed at the airport at Guatemala City, Millie and Marianne were met in baggage claim by Antonio, who was to be their driver during their stay in Guatemala. After retrieving their bags, the diminutive Antonio escorted the two women to his car for the ninety-minute trip over the mountains to Antigua. Both Millie and Marianne were lost in their thoughts during the drive through the dark, forbidding countryside. For neither the first nor the last time, Millie worried that this whole affair was just too uncertain, too fraught with strange possibilities for a middle-aged, damaged woman. She, of course, understood that riding in the dark through Central Guatemala with a strange driver and a stiff-lipped companion was no time to change her mind. Like it or not, she was committed.

Upon arriving at the Santa Clara Hotel, Millie and Marianne quickly found their rooms and retired for the night with virtually no conversation between them except to set a time to meet for breakfast.

Their breakfast the next morning began awkwardly. Millie had studied up on Guatemala and especially Antigua, a city she'd never heard of before this trip. Wishing to establish some rapport with Marianne, Millie began to share what she'd learned.

"Marianne, did you know that Antigua was once the capital of Spanish Central America? My guidebook calls it 'a city lost in time' because it was deserted for over a hundred years. I've also learned that Antigua is a UNESCO World Heritage site. Did you know that, Marianne?"

"No, I didn't. Thank you for enlightening me," came the brusque reply.

Going on, Millie related more of what she'd learned, reading aloud from her guidebook.

"Founded in 1543 by Spanish conquistadores, Antigua served as the home base for political and spiritual life in a large part of the New World. However, the sixteenth century city planners could not have imagined the discovery of plate tectonics, a science that would, in the twentieth century, explain the many volcanoes and earthquakes that continue to plague Antigua with great regularity. This is pretty interesting, isn't it?"

"Yes, it certainly is, Millie," responded Marianne, suppressing what appeared to be a yawn.

Undeterred, Millie continued reading. "As soon as the baroque churches and public buildings were completed, they seemed to tumble down as the shaking ground reduced them to their foundations. The locals of the day were certain that it was the will of God. As a result, the capital was finally moved over the mountains to what is now Guatemala City, and Antigua was abandoned to nature, becoming completely deserted for over a hundred years.

"Only in the twentieth century was the city rediscovered and revitalized to become a tourist and retirement attraction, with its amazing sixteenth and seventeenth century architecture and mild climate. Modern buildings are limited to two stories."

Once Millie finished her history lesson, there was nothing left to do but sip her coffee in silence as Marianne stared out the window of the restaurant, avoiding any eye contact.

Antonio met them after breakfast, ready to take them to the village of their first candidate, Father Victor Cardenas. In the daylight, Millie could see the beauty of Antigua, including the abundant flowers that seemed to adorn every man-made structure. The sound of roosters greeting the day, mingled with the bells of dozens of churches.

However, Antigua's beauty included cobblestone streets, which made the simple activity of walking to the car extremely challenging for Millie. As a result, it was necessary for her to wear her braces.

Antigua is surrounded by small villages like San Jose, each of which was originally the headquarters of a *finca*, or coffee plantation. These were massive estates, originally granted to upper-class settlers who had won favor with the Spanish crown. Handed down from generation to generation, each *finca* is a self-sufficient community, not unlike feudal Europe, with an aristocratic family at its center, and including a parish church, complete with a priest. Over the centuries, this system has changed little, except that in the twenty-first century, priests are in short supply, and most of the churches are deserted.

The beauty of Guatemala hides a mostly unspoken secret of class conflict. Ever since it was settled by the Spanish, the wealthy, landed class, populated by descendants of the Spanish aristocracy, has sought to keep the indigenous population in its place. Intermarriage between the two classes is rare, and with the army on the side of the ruling class, there has been little hope for the poor. The irony, of course, is that the peasant class of Guatemala today is descended from the mighty Maya, whose ancient culture is now studied, and in many ways, revered.

At times, the conflict has flared into violence. The church has mostly remained silent, though in a few cases, a local priest has stood with the poor against the army, sometimes at the cost of his life. Such was the culture into which Millie and Marianne were probing.

A fifteen-minute drive over dusty, unpaved roads led to the village of San Jose, up the slopes of one of the volcanoes that surround Antigua. Upon arrival, they initially saw no one. The entire village seemed abandoned and totally still in the steamy morning sun. Wandering down the sunbaked, unpaved street, they could see every building in the village in a matter of seconds. The only sound other than the occasional crow of a rooster was the clicking that Millie's braces made at her every step. It occurred to Millie that anyone wishing to hide couldn't find a more obscure spot than this.

The church was both beautiful and large, totally out of proportion to the population of the *finca*, which might include no more than twenty families. Millie was reminded that such churches were little more than trophies of the landed family, meant to impress their peers but never intended to be functional for the broader community.

They opened the tall wooden church door, plunging into a darkness illuminated only by several candles that had nearly burned down. As their eyes became used to the dimness, they could see an architectural marvel, with carved wooden pews and altar, faded frescoes on the walls, and paintings darkened by centuries of candle smoke.

Still, not a soul appeared. The two women walked silently through the church, paused at the altar to view the elaborate gold cross, and continued out the side door. There, they found a small vegetable garden that appeared well tended.

Suddenly, an old man shuffled out from a shed behind the church, carrying a basket of fruits and vegetables. Though his abrupt appearance startled them, he seemed quite comfortable to see strangers in the village. Smiling, he greeted them in Spanish: *"Buenos dias, senoras!"*

"Buenos dias, padre," replied Millie, exhausting most of her Spanish.

Noting that her accent gave her away, the man replied in English, "Children, what can I do for you? Are you lost?"

Without any pre-planning, Millie blurted out, "No sir, we are tourists, studying archeology at the ruins of Tikal. We heard about San Jose and this church, and we wanted to see it." *Maybe my degree in archeology might actually come in handy after all*, Millie thought to herself.

"Are you Father Cardenas?" she nervously asked. Millie knew of no other way to begin than by asking outright to see the padre. The pause that followed seemed endless to Millie, who vainly hoped that Marianne might bail her out with a smoother introduction. However, Marianne said nothing, though she appeared to be carefully scrutinizing the old man's face.

"No, children, Father Cardenas, our pastor, is in Antigua today. I am the sexton of the church, and I have worked for Father Cardenas for over forty years. Would you like to see the church?"

"Yes, of course," replied Millie, not knowing how to proceed from this setback. "But we'd also like to meet Father Cardenas, if that is possible. Is that possible?"

"Of course. My name is Juan. I will show you the church and then we will see about Father Cardenas." But then, "However I am not sure that you will be able to actually see Father Cardenas today. He is in the hospital in Antigua, you know."

Was this little man already suspicious? Was Father Cardenas ill or just visiting parishioners? Was Juan's role to protect his identity by keeping outsiders away? Millie wondered if they had already said too much and blown their cover. She tried to quiet her nerves.

Their brief tour did not reveal much more about Father Cardenas. Juan reported that Victor Cardenas had grown up in Spain, had been ordained in his twenties, and was now in his eighties. Juan, another diminutive Guatemalan, was also elderly but spry enough to take care of the church and tend its garden.

It was time to go. But Millie would not leave without asking again to see Father Cardenas. "Come back tomorrow," Juan replied, giving them a vague hope that their trip might not be in vain.

They did come back the next day, and the next, and the next.

After three fruitless days of driving with Antonio up the dusty road to San Jose, and three pleasant but unproductive conversations with Juan, Millie decided on a different tack. Upon expressing the usual disappointment upon missing Father Cardenas (excuses ranged from visits to the hospital, a shopping excursion to Antigua and a visit to the bishop in Guatemala City), Millie explained to Juan that they must leave Antigua and return to Tikal. This was good-bye. *Adios!*

"What are you *doing*?" Marianne asked in the car, her voice tinged with frustration. "We can't leave; we've got to see Victor Cardenas."

"I have a plan," Millie responded. "We could go on like this for days, driving up to San Jose and waiting for Juan's latest excuse as to why Father Cardenas is not available. Tomorrow, we'll make a surprise attack!"

As planned, the fourth day saw Millie and Marianne wait until almost dark before returning to San Jose. Hopefully, their surprise timing would pay off.

Entering the church in the twilight, they spotted a shadowy figure at the front by the altar. At first, he seemed to be statue-like, as if he were deep in private contemplation. Then, he began to slowly and deliberately move, extinguishing all but one of the candles. Her heart pounding, Millie cried out in her most reverent but clear voice, "Father Cardenas?"

The distinguished-looking elderly priest turned and looked them over for a long moment. Juan had briefed him on the two women, including their expected departure. "*Senoras?* You have returned, *si?*"

"Yes, Father, we so much wanted to meet you."

"Yes. And I you. But it is getting late. Can I offer you some soup?"

And so the conversation began, awkwardly. Juan soon joined them, also surprised at their return. It would have been impolite, however, for him to ask why they came back.

The corn soup, thick Guatemalan tortillas and red wine were simple but filling. They ate in the small rectory where Father Cardenas lived, along with Juan.

"Father, we have heard of you in the United States," Millie began hesitatingly. It was important to carefully move into the real reason for their visit. "Your 1985 letter to Rome was circulated and has won much praise in the USA."

The letter Millie referred to was one of the matches to the Gospel of John. It covered the violence that raged in Guatemala during the 1980s and '90s, appealing to Rome to take a stand for the peasant population.

"Your writing is very eloquent," Millie went on.

"Ah, I only wish it had been more eloquent," Cardenas answered. "Perhaps some positive action might have come from it. Instead, only more disappearances and more deaths. I could have done more. I should have done more. But I failed. And as a result, more suffering."

"Father, was your letter originally a sermon that you preached?"

"Yes, my child, it was. Actually, I preached that sermon at the cathedral in Antigua. It was well received and I made it into the letter that went to Rome. It also appeared in local newspapers. Our bishop at the time approved it first, of course. He, unfortunately, is now dead, replaced by another who is not so inclined to upset Rome. But why do you ask?"

Millie was making progress but was afraid to push too far. "If you have more of your sermons, we'd love to read them. Do you think that is possible?"

"Perhaps, but I do not generally save them. I might have a few. You are welcome to have them, as I seldom preach these days. You see, Rome was not pleased with the publicity that came from my letter."

Father Cardenas went on for the next two hours, recounting his history as a priest who stood for the peasant class in a country still mostly ruled by an aristocracy, one that had strong connections in Rome. Millie's admiration for him grew as she listened, and she couldn't help but connect him to her image of the Apostle John, who Jesus had nicknamed, along with his brother James, the "Sons of Thunder." As she listened, Millie could almost hear a younger Father Cardenas "thunder" as he preached.

She could see, also, that though he stood with the poor, he was not of the poor. Father Cardenas was clearly well educated. He projected a dignity that seemed to elevate him above his humble parish, but without arrogance or pretension.

"You must excuse an old man, I have gone on far too long, haven't I?" he finally asked. "You have been very gracious to listen to my ramblings."

"Not at all, Father, but it's getting late, and we must go." Before leaving, Millie returned to the subject of Father Cardenas' other sermons.

"We would love to read any of your other sermons. May we return tomorrow?" This was more than she had dreamed that they might accomplish.

"Of course. Now tell me why you are so interested in a simple priest and his sermons from long ago."

6

Millie had not expected the pointblank question from Father Cardenas. After an awkward pause, all she could think to say was, "Father Cardenas, you may not realize the impact your letter made in the US. When we learned of your location here in San Jose, we just had to meet you."

Father Cardenas did not respond to her obviously contrived answer. Millie and Marianne quickly made their exit.

Back at the hotel, the two women plotted their strategy for the next day. Marianne was convinced that they had their man.

"Clearly, his letter matches. He's in an obscure place, alone with a guardian who shoos away anyone who tries to get too close. The only thing I can't figure is why he would risk sending that letter to Rome. The publicity might have led to his discovery."

"But remember," injected Millie, "That was back in the 1980's. He would have had no idea of the technology of today. Even today, he probably is still unaware of our computer programs and our ability to match writings across the centuries. And of course, he was passionate for a cause and perhaps willing to take a risk."

"The big puzzle for me," continued Millie, "is if he's actually aware that he is John. Perhaps he doesn't even know. Perhaps he thinks he's just some ordinary parish priest in a remote place in Guatemala, with all previous memory totally erased."

"That's an interesting possibility," responded Marianne, "Which if true, should make it all the easier to get really close to him."

Millie's phone showed a missed call from Randall. "When are you coming home?" were the only words in the message.

She was not surprised that he said nothing more. She phoned him back and told him of the trip. Millie had shared little about this project with Randall, keeping as much as possible in compliance with Douglas Parks' instructions.

"So what are you actually doing in Guatemala?" He tried as hard as he could to sound disinterested, merely curious.

"Well," she replied, "We're looking for the lost city of El Dorado. We hope to find a tribe of pygmies here who trace their roots back to the Stone Age." Millie was never very good at sarcasm.

"Okay," he responded, "I guess you're just not going to tell me what you are doing. I had thought you were pursuing some figure from the past, someone who should be long dead. But, of course, you claim that this person is still alive after two thousand years."

"Oh yes, I forgot, we're doing that too."

Father Cardenas was not in San Jose when they returned the next morning. As usual, Juan, the sexton, received them in the dim sanctuary.

"Welcome, my children. I am afraid that Father has been called away again. He so much wished to see you once more before your departure."

"We, too, are disappointed," replied Millie, "but we understand. He must be quite busy, even in this remote parish."

"Yes, of course," Juan went on, "but he did want you to have these." He handed over several sheets of yellowed paper, containing handwritten sermons, evidently from long ago.

"We are so thankful, Juan. Please pass on our gratitude to Father Cardenas. If he would like, we can make copies of these and mail back the originals to him."

"That is a gracious offer, my child, but it will not be necessary. He truly wants you to have them for whatever purpose or use you may have in mind."

After leaving most of the previous evening's conversation to Millie, Marianne suddenly spoke up. "Juan," she asked, "Does Father Cardenas receive many visitors here? I mean besides yourself, is anyone else frequently around?"

"No, my child," came the response, "We live very much in isolation here, in peace. The members of the family, the owners of the estate, are seldom in Guatemala, and the workers are usually out in the coffee fields. Unfortunately, only a few of the *viejos*, the old ones, come to the church. Our sanctuary is usually dark, as you see, but the light of Christ still shines in our hearts, and that True Light can never be extinguished. That light is truly eternal and we live for the day when he will return and his light will shine in the hearts of all peoples."

Marianne probed a bit further: "Doesn't Father keep any kind of regular schedule? I mean aren't there certain days or times when he is always here?" Millie was increasingly uncomfortable with these questions, which seemed to go too far beyond their objective for a first visit.

"We live simple lives here," he replied. "I go once a week to Antigua to purchase what we need, and Father occasionally visits the bishop in Guatemala City. Once, he was a frequent guest at the cathedral in Antigua, but now, he is considered too old to conduct mass. I hope that I have answered your questions," and he rose to usher them out.

"We are so grateful for this opportunity to visit you and Father Cardenas," Millie spoke affectionately as she had become fond of these two old men. "Your hospitality is a wonderful example and does credit to your church and your country."

"We are pleased to have visitors as pleasant as you," he responded, and as they walked toward the sunlight coming through the cracks in the church door, he added, "We are an outpost, a lonely place where the true word is honored and lived out to the best of our abilities.

"All of us are wounded in many ways," he went on, "but in our case, the wounds we have suffered have opened many doors to witness to the one whose wounds went beyond anything that we might experience. We are one with the poor, the people of this village."

He did not explain what he meant about their wounds, but continued, speaking directly to Millie. "I have noticed that you, too, are wounded, my child, and that walking is difficult for you, especially here on our uneven streets and steep mountain paths. I hope this has not been too much of a burden. And I am sure that the one who was wounded for our sins will provide for you an opportunity to use your wounds for good."

Millie was unsure how to respond, or if a response was even needed. But she felt that she could say almost anything to this simple man of wisdom, "Thank you for your concern, Juan; I'm beginning to believe that this wound, my disability, will someday open a door for me to serve in a way that I can't yet see."

The words coming out of Millie's mouth were surprising to her as she said them; she had not previously had these thoughts. As she listened to her own words, it was almost as if she and Juan were speaking a new language, one of the spirit and not of the everyday world.

"Yes, the reasons for our suffering will always appear eventually, even if not for a long time. Peace and blessings to you both. Good-bye." And he disappeared back into the dark church.

Antonio was in the car, ready to take them back to the hotel, to pack, and then to the airport in Guatemala City. Marianne was anxious to leave but Millie felt a longing to stay. She knew that they must go but in her heart, she hoped for a reason to return to San Jose.

Once in the car, Millie voiced her discomfort with Marianne's probing questions. She couldn't keep from asking: "What were you trying to find out by asking all those questions?"

"Only that we will need to return here sometime, and get him alone," Marianne responded, brusquely. "And if we do, we'll need to know when is the best time to find him, and to isolate him from Juan's protection." She did not explain further and there were few words between them all the way back to the U.S.

The flight home gave Millie a chance to reflect on their time in Antigua. She had truly grown fond of the two old men, especially Juan, who had spent so many hours with them. Intentionally or not, he had gently but very effectively kept Marianne and Millie away from Father

Cardenas. But even as he did so, he showed genuine affection for the two American women, whose mission was so clearly not what they had represented.

If Victor Cardenas was, in fact, the Apostle John, perhaps he would need a protector like Juan. And while Juan was, in fact, very pleasant, he had presented a formidable obstacle that neither Millie nor Marianne had been able to penetrate, other than for the one evening with Father Cardenas.

Millie also pondered Marianne's final interrogation of Juan. *She seemed to push too far, perhaps giving away our purpose. Was there a hidden agenda with her questions?*

Something in Marianne's whole attitude seemed dark in a way that Millie couldn't quite grasp. And Millie was unable to make any headway in probing into Marianne's motives.

At their debriefing meeting with Dr. Chandler and Douglas Parks, Marianne did a surprising about-face. While Millie could believe that Father Cardenas might truly be the Apostle John, Marianne took the opposite position, despite her original belief that they had their man.

"I believe we can just go on to other possibilities. He is not John," she told Chandler and Parks. "We don't need to return to Antigua."

"Millie, what about you?" Dr. Chandler asked.

"While I agree with Marianne that we need to look at other possibilities, I'm not ready to count Father Cardenas out of consideration," she said, wondering about Marianne's change of heart. "We really were able to spend very little time with him because of Juan, the sexton of his church. He did such a good job of keeping us away from Father Cardenas. And that fact must mean something, which might be that Father Cardenas really is John and desires to stay out of the public eye."

"Okay," concluded Parks, careful not to share with them the results from the other members of the team. "It's still early in the process. We'll keep open the possibility for Father Cardenas, but we'll certainly want to go on with the remainder of the candidates. Oh, and by the way, we've run the sermons he gave you through our software. They all match the writings of the Apostle John. Without exception."

The meeting broke up. Millie was anxious to have a private conversation with Dr. Chandler, who she knew would share more than she had heard from Parks.

"Yes, Millie, I can tell you more," confided Dr. Chandler as they met over coffee.

"We've heard from one other team, from a visit to the English candidate by Hans Oltorf and Hugh Matthews. There, they met with a solicitor for a bank, a man who has written extensively over a forty year career. It seems that some of his writings match the John profile, while others do not. It's a bit puzzling, to tell you the truth. We expected more consistency and to be frank, it places the entire program in a tricky place. You see, a mixed result will keep the door open for all kinds of negative interpretations. For example, it could be viewed that our findings are nothing more than coincidence and our results too inconclusive. The foundation funding this project wants a definite and airtight answer."

"So what happens next?" she asked, wondering if the project was essentially over.

"A second team will return to England for a closer look. And in the meantime, we want you to go to France with Monsignor Morelli."

"But Dr. Chandler, I did such a poor job in Guatemala. We spent so little time with Father Cardenas. Don't you want to send someone more qualified?"

"Definitely not, Millie. You did fine in Guatemala. We'll send a second team back there to dig a little deeper. What you came back with, the sermons he gave you, were just what we needed. As Parks told you, they have been run through the software and have produced additional matches with the writings of the Apostle John. This is very encouraging, but of course, we have only a very small sample. Now is the time to be patient."

After Millie's experience in Antigua, returning home was difficult.

"I can't really tell you anything about what I did," she told Randall, covering her mixed emotions as best she could. She would not share her experience with Randall, partly because this experience was hers and hers alone, and partly because she was convinced that she'd failed in Antigua.

"Well, your crazy little trip is of no concern to me, anyway," was his curt response, and the conversation was over.

When she couldn't sleep, Millie found herself continuing to wonder about Father Cardenas, and also about Juan. Why would Juan be so protective of Father Cardenas, unless he truly was the Apostle John? *Surely,* she thought, *he must be the man we're searching for.* It all added up: the remote location, the protector, and the sermons that matched the Gospel of John. Perhaps they should have just confronted him with what they knew and what they could deduce. And if they had done so, would he have admitted who he was?

Millie returned to her daily prayer time, but it now seemed flat and lifeless. Something had changed, though she was not sure what or how.

"What has changed, is you!" Sister Camilla remarked when Millie visited her at the Abbey. "You've embarked on a spiritual adventure and you are under attack!"

It sounded far too dramatic to Millie. She wasn't sure that she believed in such things as forces of evil, spiritual attacks and the like.

"You are being pulled into a deeper confrontation with spiritual forces," the wrinkled nun went on. "Arm yourself for a battle. Something is coming that you cannot foresee."

"Yes," responded Millie, "perhaps you're right. It feels like I'm entering a long, dark tunnel. I can't see anything ahead and it's very upsetting."

"Just remember," advised Sister Camilla, "Our Lord does some of His best work in the dark. Don't be afraid of uncertainty, or doubts. Just open yourself to his leading, even if you can't see where you are going."

She went on: "I can see that you are disappointed in yourself about something that has happened since our last visit. You wish to know something that you've been kept from knowing, and you feel in the dark. Millie, there is a deeper knowing, one that lives in mystery and paradox. You are not in the center of it, but can find yourself out on the fringes. What's in the center? Something bigger and deeper than any of us can fully know. We can touch it and it can touch us. We can interact with it and it can interact with us. We can even join it without owning it or sensing it fully.

"Millie, you are being drawn closer to the center, and you must not be afraid to allow it to pull you into something not of your own making. Whatever it is, it is an experience that is outside of your control. And any attempt to own it or manage it will be futile."

Sort of like pulling a dangling thread, thought Millie.

7

In the shadows, the jeep drove slowly up the winding road to San Jose, headlights off. It was twilight. The four armed men, dressed in military fatigues, rode silently, mentally rehearsing their assignment, which had been planned soon after the two American women left Guatemala. The stillness was broken only by the hum of the jeep's engine and the crunching sound its tires made on the uneven, rocky road.

They stopped in front of the church, which appeared deserted. A breathless moment passed while they collected themselves for their appointed task.

Standing alone by the altar, Father Cardenas turned to greet the men as they slowly entered through the wooden door of the dimly lit church. With pistols already drawn, they walked toward him, their boots echoing in unison on the stone floor. Shadows of the men played grotesquely on the stone walls as they progressed in single file toward Father Cardenas. Unafraid of detection, their faces were clearly visible in the candlelight; nor did they fear that he might run from them, even though their purpose could not be mistaken.

Father Cardenas imagined that this day might eventually come; he just didn't know when. But it was immediately clear to him as soon as he saw the men enter the church. Without a doubt, sending four armed men for this task was meant to make a statement, to ensure that everyone would know and fear the power behind their mission.

"Welcome, my sons, to this time of prayer," Father Cardenas greeted them. "You are just in time for vespers. We must all pray for forgiveness, mustn't we? Won't you join me?" He knew their answer would come swiftly. He was prepared for his fate, but genuinely worried about theirs.

Without answering, they surrounded Father Cardenas, towering over him at point blank range, ready to strike. The silence begged to be broken.

Just then, Juan entered through the side door, and immediately sizing up what was happening, he sought to head off the inevitable.

"Noooo, noooo, do not do this!" he implored, feebly struggling with the closest soldier, who blocked his way. "You do not know what you are doing! Do not do this evil thing! This is wrong! Stop this!"

The soldier roughly pushed Juan aside, and he lost his balance, falling hard on the stone floor. As he fell, his head hit an iron candle stand, causing a deep gash. Bleeding from the gash and now semi-conscious, he continued to moan, "Do not do this, do not do this!" But he was unable to get up and resist any further.

"We don't want you, old man, you are worth nothing to us," sneered the soldier. He turned back to Father Cardenas, who was by now kneeling on the floor, tightly gripping a crucifix. It was not clear if he was kneeling in prayer or in submission to his fate.

One shot at close range would have satisfied their assignment. But this was a public killing, a ceremony of terror meant to attract attention and make a statement. So, after a momentary pause, all four opened fire, emptying their magazines, shell casings crazily bouncing off the floor. For several seconds the deafening noise echoed off the stone walls of the church, then faded into a somber quiet. Devoid of emotion, the four men stared at Father Cardenas for a long moment as the smoke cleared, viewing the visceral consequence of their task, but unaware of its deeper significance.

Their work done, the soldiers holstered their pistols and quietly retreated toward the door. As they did, each one carefully stepped over Juan, who continued to softly moan. The stilled figure of Father Victor Cardenas, now an unrecognizable mass of blood and flesh, was left by the altar, his hands still gripping the crucifix. The crimson stains on the church floor would never be erased.

■ ■ ■

Once they had landed at Charles DeGaulle airport and turned on their cell phones, both Monsignor Morelli and Millie read messages from Douglas Parks instructing them to immediately catch the next flight home. No details were offered in the brief message. They quickly arranged a flight back to the U.S.

Their debriefing with Parks and Dr. Chandler shook Millie to the core. The assassination of Father Cardenas, shocking as it was, was only the beginning. Tears filled her eyes as Millie remembered the sweet-natured priest, and she wondered about the fate of Juan.

"We're now forced to tell you more about this project," began Parks, hesitatingly, "things that we dared not share with you before, but must tell you now in light of the murder of Father Cardenas." He trembled as he spoke, his prior focus on confidentiality making it especially hard for him to reveal what he had to say.

"Start from the beginning," urged Dr. Chandler and Parks nodded in agreement.

"Before assembling the team we now have," began Parks, "Dr. Chandler and I made what you might call a trial run; we had to make sure that we were on solid ground before bringing in the broader team that you are now a member of.

"Our trial run," he continued, "was with the first person to match the Gospel of John in the software. He is a professor at Ashwood Seminary in Kentucky. He is also a Presbyterian pastor of some note. His books are widely read, and he is a frequent speaker at spiritual conferences.

"Of course, he was surprised when we came to him with our results, never dreaming that he could be detected in this manner. He had no knowledge of our computing power and he was virtually unprotected, meaning that he had no 'Juan' as a gatekeeper and showed little concern for his anonymity. Oh, and I should tell you that this was about six months ago.

"We had strong evidence based on matches from our software, which was still being tested at the time. You might imagine that he was, to us, an easy target in that he was local and thus accessible. He is also a prolific writer. As a result, there were many matches in the database. We were sure that we had our man; certain that he was, in fact, the Apostle John. It seemed likely that any further searching would be unnecessary, other than to disqualify any others whose writings also matched the writings of John."

Parks went on, his forehead beginning to glisten with perspiration, his voice beginning to rise in a nervousness that Millie had not noticed before.

"We asked him why he was so unafraid of detection. And of course, we asked if he was, in fact, John the Apostle. His response surprised us."

At this, Dr. Chandler broke in, "He is not the Apostle John, although he could have fooled anyone, you see. What we learned is that he is a 'plant' of sorts, a decoy who has been given the ability to write as John wrote, and to appear in all other respects as if he were, in fact, the Apostle John. He explained, you see, that throughout history, John's appearances have always coincided with multiple decoys, designed to protect his identity from outside forces who might want to harm him. And that is why we found concurrent matches in our database, and it's also why we must examine all of the candidates. Most of them – theoretically, all but one of them, in fact -- will turn out to be decoys, planted to keep safe the true Apostle John."

"But why would anyone wish to harm the Apostle John? Why is there a need for decoys?" asked Millie.

"The system of decoys worked flawlessly, you see, for almost two thousand years," Dr. Chandler went on excitedly, disregarding her question. "But now, with the increased computing power and the advent of rapid global transportation, it has become easier to penetrate this system to quickly rule out the decoys and possibly find the true John."

"Yes," Parks continued, "the decoys worked until now. Why were they needed? Let's just say that we are not the only people searching for John. There are others. And over the centuries, these others, with evil intent, have also searched for John, and continue to search for him, even today. Think back to the words of Jesus in the passage from John 21:

> *"…if he is to remain until I come again, what is that to you?"*

"Most theologians believe that Jesus' quote refers to John, the author of the Gospel of John and the one who was called 'the disciple whom Jesus loved.'"

"The implication of this," interrupted Dr. Chandler, "was that John's earthly death will coincide with the second coming of Christ. And the evil forces, who seek to discredit the prophecy, reasoned that if John could be killed, and Christ did not immediately return as predicted, it would prove the prophecy wrong. And in so doing it would raise doubts over other scripture as well, weakening the faith of believers around the world. So their intent is to kill him. Plus, frankly, they're just plain evil."

Millie's head was spinning. "So," she began slowly, "this man whom you found, the seminary professor, is not John, but is supposed to be a sort of stand-in for John? His job is to attract attention to himself, in order to distract forces of evil from the real John? Doesn't he realize that he might get killed in the process?"

"Yes," responded Parks, "he does, and that is his choice, a risk he is willing to take for his faith. Think about it, though, the feeling of a believer to be chosen for such a mission! And let me say that historically, we have found only a few cases of a decoy perishing in a premature death. One, from the sixth century, a German monk, who it seems was pushed off a bridge, and another, from the sixteenth century, who died under torture in the Spanish Inquisition. Exact reasons for their deaths are, of course, hard to determine, looking back from hundreds of years later."

"But we are reasonably certain," added Dr. Chandler, that forces of evil, going all the way back to the first century, have sought to kill all of Jesus' closest disciples. And church tradition tells us that they were, indeed, quite successful. All were martyred, sometimes in very gruesome ways. All that is, except one disciple: John."

"Then," asked Millie, "was Father Cardenas simply another decoy, meant to draw the enemy away from the real Apostle John? If so, he certainly paid a high price."

"We'll not know the answer to that, Millie, until we examine the other candidates," responded Dr. Chandler. "In the meantime, we must assume that, unless we see Christ coming on the clouds, Father Cardenas was a decoy, a sacrificial lamb, living at risk of being slain."

"And that also must mean," injected Monsignor Morelli, "that the forces wishing to kill John will continue to search for him."

"Forces of evil?" asked Millie. "Who are they?"

"We are researching that question, Millie, and finding little evidence of an organized group," responded Dr. Chandler. "Clearly, the assassination of Father Cardenas was meant to look like a group of extremists from the Guatemalan army, taking matters into their own hands with an intransigent priest.

"But that's not factual. The reality is that there has been an uneasy peace between the Guatemalan army and the peasant class for over fifteen years now. This assassination was instead a professional hit, carried out by mercenaries who probably had no idea why they were killing Father Cardenas."

"Can we trace back to see who authorized and arranged this tragedy?" asked Monsignor Morelli.

"Yes, we are working on that, but have no answers yet," replied Parks. "And there is one more thing, perhaps the hardest part to share with you."

Wondering what that could possibly be after so many terrible revelations, Millie wasn't sure that she wanted to hear any more.

"You remember," began Parks, "that we emphasized confidentiality from the beginning, keeping all details of our work to the smallest possible group. But now, in light of this terrible tragedy, we can't escape the likelihood that the murderers knew of Father Cardenas, and of our project."

"They must have known," added Dr. Chandler, "but how could they know? We can only assume that knowledge of your visit and the identity of Father Cardenas were leaked outside of our team. It's very possible that the evil forces that we must investigate have access to the inner workings of our team; in effect, a person on the inside."

There was a moment of shocked silence as Millie and Monsignor Morelli processed what they were hearing.

"What must we do now?" asked Monsignor Morelli. "It would seem that we must tighten our security and move to not only investigate the murder of Father Cardenas, but also to quickly visit the remaining candidates."

"Yes," replied Parks. "The first step is to return to Antigua to investigate further, to search for any witnesses to the murder, including its planning."

"Witnesses, yes, of course. Juan!" exclaimed Millie. "He did survive, didn't he?"

"We don't know," responded Dr. Chandler. "We've inquired at all the local hospitals. All we can determine is that Juan has disappeared."

"Then I must go back to Antigua and find him." Her interest in returning was driven as much by her affection for Juan as for the need to investigate the murder of Father Cardenas.

"No Millie," replied Dr. Chandler. "We can send others to Antigua. We will find Juan and hope that he can shed light on the assassination. But you and Monsignor Morelli must return to France. It's important to reach our candidate there before others can find him, and we might already be too late. You must go to France."

"Yes," responded Millie, already fearing a repeat of her experience in Guatemala. "I will go to France. But I've had enough murders, for now, so please, no more."

8

Millie was shaken by the terrible revelations surrounding the murder of Father Cardenas. She had only one day before she must leave again on her next assignment, with Monsignor Morelli, to France. Millie needed to pull herself together.

In light of the strain on her marriage, Millie felt deprived of a support system that would carry her through such a difficult time. And so, after briefly re-connecting with Randall, she visited the Abbey and Sister Camilla.

"Sister Camilla, it's this project that I've been pulled into. I don't think I can continue. It's demanding more of me than I can give. I was never right for this and should have realized that before I started. I want out." Millie's hands were shaking as she poured out her heart to the tiny nun.

"My child," comforted Sister Camilla, "don't you realize that you are in very good company?" She would not offer an opinion on Millie's statement about "wanting out."

"In good company? What do you mean?"

"Think about the giants of our faith," Camilla went on, "starting with Abraham the liar who prostituted his own wife; Moses, the imposter who was sure that God had chosen the wrong man, down to St. Peter, the uneducated fisherman who more than once quit on Jesus, and whose character flaws could fill a book. And what about St. Paul, a cold-blooded killer? You think yourself unlikely for your project? Think about these so-called giants of our faith and remember how unlikely they were. And think about what made the difference for them."

Taken aback, all Millie could think was to ask, "Well, what *did* make the difference?"

"It wasn't ability, or in some cases, even the desire to serve or lead. What made the difference for them was the Spirit of Christ, calling, equipping and encouraging in the face of daunting odds, repeated failures and staggering opposition. When these individuals stopped trying to achieve and lead on their own, and when they learned obedience to the one who called them, they were able to find themselves, their true selves. And once they responded to their calling, they were able to serve with great ability. Millie, you must look deeper within yourself to find that same ability, an ability that was planted there before you were born.

"Millie, I know nothing of your project. But I do know this: you have been called; and your calling is as sure as anything I know. You look ahead and hope to see what might happen next. But you will never see it coming. Instead, you will suddenly be confronted with an unforeseen opportunity to make a difference, and you will respond. I have faith in you. I believe in you. You will overcome what you think are your handicaps and weaknesses, and find that instead of problems, they are actually assets. Your wounds and shortcomings are just what our Lord uses to work with, to produce the fruit that he calls us to."

It took some time for Millie to digest the words of Sister Camilla. Nothing she had ever heard sounded like what Sister Camilla told her. No one since Father Vlacek had expressed so much faith in her. That affirmation sank deep into her inner being. And somewhere inside, in her inner self, Millie found a new resolve. And that resolve told her that before departing for France, she must have a conversation with Randall. It would be difficult.

"You wonder what I'm doing, flying all over the world for this strange project, don't you?" She began. "Why *am* I doing this? I know that you'll use your impeccable logic and tell me that what I'm doing is crazy. Won't you? And maybe it is crazy, I'm willing to admit to that. Maybe it is.

"But before you judge me, and before you condemn me, let me tell you that your indiscretions with your co-worker (whom she refused to name) might have actually encouraged me to take this on."

Randall's typical defense in an argument was to avoid openly reacting in any way to what Millie said, to keep his composure no matter what. But when she uncovered the "elephant in the room," his extra-marital activities, he could not hide his surprise and shame. It seemed that his impregnable protective shell might be broken, or at least dented just a bit. His face showed it. Randall was speechless.

"You have no idea how you've hurt me," she went on, letting the words flow unfiltered from her heart. "We don't have the time to go into your affair just now, but we will. And I can tell you that ironically, my 'strange project' has given me a release from sitting at home, wondering where you are and who you're with. This project has been a boost to my self-image, just when you were tearing it down with your 'business trips.' And if nothing else, I'm grateful for that.

"Let me tell you," she continued, "I don't really know why I'm doing this project, but it has a hold on me and I simply cannot let go of it. For the first time in my almost fifty years, I'm doing something that is way outside my comfort zone. It isn't pretty; in fact, it is quite messy, and it's not going well at all. And I think, and actually, I'm pretty sure, that it's all my fault.

"But in some strange way, I'm being fed spiritually. I'm coming alive in a way that I never dreamed of. You probably won't understand this, but I'm trying to be faithful to something that I can't explain. I know that you think I must be crazy in doing all of this. It's not logical, I know that. So go ahead and call me crazy. But I'm also crazy enough to hope that you'll be faithful, faithful enough to hang in with me to the end of this. And support me as best you can."

There was a long silence as he processed her impassioned speech. She was always the direct one, the one who could speak her mind with no collateral damage. He, on the other hand, must be careful. Randall always tried to be correct, to calculate what he said before he said it, and to speak in a way that could not provoke an argument that he might lose.

But this time, with her knowledge of his indiscretions, he was stripped to the bone. His intellect deserted him and he was unarmed against her direct, yet vulnerable attack. In a way, Randall was reminded that he did appreciate her, and as much as he was capable of, he did love her, almost because she was so much the person that he would have liked to be.

All he could respond was, "Millie, you are right. I don't understand what you're doing. It makes no sense and it seems destructive to you and to our relationship. I wonder what is the end game of all this? I mean, what are you producing? Are you producing anything at all? Anything for the good of anyone? It just seems that you're traveling to strange places and trying to uncover something that should remain hidden, or which never existed in the first place.

"But whatever has happened, and regardless of what I think about this calling that seems to have such a hold on you, I do want you to know that I continue to place great value on our marriage; I want it to work. But honestly, I don't know how. Maybe I'm jealous of what you are doing, or at least a little envious. Maybe I've been a great failure at understanding you. Maybe I've kept myself in a cave of my own making. I should work on that. But I can tell you that whatever crazy thing you're doing, I will wait for you. I will be faithful. I promise. But please don't expect me to understand what you're doing and why you're doing it."

The conversation ended there, with neither of them feeling good about it.

Before packing for France, Millie phoned her children, both of whom were still off at college. Satisfying herself that Paul and Leslie were okay, she readied herself for the next trip.

■ ■ ■

Millie settled into her seat, ready for the flight that would take Monsignor Morelli and her through Paris, on to Toulouse and finally, into the foothills of the Pyrenees, near the Spanish border . Morelli, who at thirty-five was at least ten years her junior, asked her to simply call him "Frank." She liked this priest who seemed so approachable and easy to know.

Their destination was a retreat center, called Naissance, southwest of Toulouse and east of Lourdes. The center was founded in the 1960's by an inter-denominational evangelical group. Pilgrims came from around the world for week-long conferences aimed at unity in the church, and at revitalizing the faith in Western Europe, where secular humanism had effectively replaced organized religion.

Charles Boutte, a youth leader at the center, was a native of Algeria, of mixed French and Algerian ancestry. He had been recruited to Naissance six years earlier. His history prior to the center was a bit fuzzy. He was their target.

Charles had written extensively, especially on evangelical topics. Many of his essays had been published in the center's monthly newsletter and posted to the center's website. More recently, he had taken to social media, blogging frequently and interactively with a wide network of followers. Virtually all his writings matched those of the Apostle John.

Boutte, a hiker in his off hours, had also served as a guide for pilgrims making the trip to Santiago de Compostela, a popular pilgrimage site in the Galician countryside of northwest Spain. Since the ninth century, Santiago was, after Rome, the most frequented pilgrim's destination for the faithful. The Naissance Center was a stopping point on one of the many paths crossing France, and converging at San Sebastian, just across the Spanish border, the beginning of the final stretch of the pilgrimage.

Millie and Frank discussed the best way to introduce themselves to Charles. As she'd learned in Antigua, the introduction was the most awkward part of their assignment. Hopefully, this time, there would be no protector like Juan, who for the most part had kept Father Cardenas out of reach.

They agreed that the Santiago pilgrimage presented the easiest opportunity for a safe introduction, one that would not arouse suspicion. Actually, the more she read about the pilgrimage, the more curious Millie became about the possibility of walking it herself. But, or course, that would have to wait, at least for now, as they planned their introduction to Boutte.

Claiming to represent a group interested in the pilgrimage, they'd want to investigate in detail, scoping out the terrain, climate, etc. Millie could make good use of her braces, offering that several members of the group might have handicaps such as hers, and would need to know if they could navigate the trail.

This approach enabled them to avoid the type of unannounced visit that had been so difficult in Antigua. Millie had made an appointment with Charles, and he was expecting them. Hopefully, this would go smoothly and they'd spend enough time with Charles to determine if he was their man.

It started out beautifully. Charles personally greeted them at the center's reception office and even offered them accommodations on site. Politely refusing, they nevertheless felt very welcomed and relieved that he seemed to suspect nothing of their true purpose. Their first conversation centered on his role, especially his guiding groups on the path to Santiago.

"The pilgrimage to Santiago was once a life-long ambition for the faithful," he explained. "In medieval times, people would travel all across Europe, often taking years at a time and frequently in danger from bandits and disease. It was known as the Way of St. James, or *Camino de Santiago*, and its symbol was the scallop shell, a badge worn by pilgrims and one still seen today on the route."

"It would be wonderful," began Frank, "if we could see part of the trail, to determine its suitability for our group."

"Of course," replied Charles, "I will have one of our associates drive you out as close to the trail as you can get via car, and then you can get out at several spots and see for yourselves."

At this unacceptable answer, Millie, using her inborn gift of naïve candor, asked, "Charles, it would be so much better if you could take the time to show us yourself. After all, we'll certainly want you as our guide if we book the trip. Would that be asking too much?"

Charles easily replied, "Of course, where is my hospitality? Certainly, I will take you myself."

Next morning, bright and early, Charles was at their inn in the little village adjacent to the center, waiting to pick them up in his four-wheel-drive SUV. However, he was not alone, for in the front seat with him was his associate, Claudine. Millie couldn't help wondering if she might be another protector, like Juan had been for Father Cardenas.

She thought, *Oh boy, here we go again!*

9

Millie and Frank had hoped to get Charles Boutte alone, thinking that the tour of the *Camino de Santiago* would be the perfect opportunity. However, his companion, Claudine, seemed to complicate their approach.

"Let me explain," began Charles. "Once a week, we must check the trails around the center, so that hikers can be sure to find them unobstructed by snow, ice, fallen trees or the like. Claudine, who is a veteran hiker and trainer, accompanies me and helps to clear the path."

Claudine, an athletic twenty-five-ish blond, sat in the front seat next to Charles. They actually made an attractive couple, Millie thought, noting Claudine's Nordic appearance in contrast with Charles' dark Algerian good looks.

Claudine was clothed in full hiking gear and to Millie's dismay, Claudine was also armed with what appeared to be a high-powered rifle. She let Charles do the talking.

"The path to San Sebastian avoids the peaks of the Pyrenees as much as possible," Charles went on. "However, we can drive up into the foothills, going high enough to offer you a view from above. You'll be able to see many miles of the path, so that you can get a feel for the elevation and terrain. Is this what you wish to see?"

"Yes," replied Frank, asking "By the way, does the *Tour de France* come anywhere near here?"

"Good question," replied Charles. "Yes, it does. However, the *Tour* follows paved roads that are not too far from here. We'll be following un-paved roads and in some cases, little more than rough paths up the steeper slopes."

Sure enough, Charles suddenly steered the SUV off of the pavement and onto what appeared to be a trail leading up a steep incline. "Hold on," he shouted over the engine's roar, "from here on, you will need to keep your seat belts tightly fastened."

The temperature became noticeably cooler as they ascended, and the valley below, where the Naissance Center was located, retreated in their view. They could look up and see snow on the peaks and in the crevasses that had not seen sunlight since the previous summer.

"If you look to your right," he went on, "you will see the *Camino de Santiago* following that stream below. It will proceed due west for some distance, keeping to the valleys and where possible, following streams. Every so often, you'll see a small village where pilgrims might stop for refreshments or lodging."

The road was not really a road at all but was little more than a cleared path, and true to Charles' prediction, they did encounter fallen branches and even an occasional fallen tree. These obstacles caused them to stop while Charles and Claudine got out to clear the path. Millie noticed that Claudine kept her rifle close by, assuming that it might be needed in case a wild creature of some kind crossed their path. Millie had not considered the need to study the wildlife of the Pyrenees.

They drove on, the road becoming even more primitive as they went. Soon, they found themselves on narrow mountain paths leading upward through passes with sheer drops to the valley below. By now it was quite cold and began to softly rain.

Entering a small meadow, they stopped and broke out a hamper with sandwiches and beer. Millie stepped out, slipped on the wet ground and started to fall. She had not worn her braces, assuming that she would stay in the car and that the path would be much more civilized than it had turned out to be. Frank caught and steadied her until she got her footing.

Charles, noticing her difficulty offered, "The *Camino* path is much easier than this, Millie. It does have its ups and downs so someone with your condition might want assistance. But it can be navigated, though some perseverance will be required."

"Yes," replied Millie, "perseverance. I've been told that I have plenty of that."

"The *Camino*," Charles went on, "goes past Bayonne and actually crosses the mountains near the coast, so that the pass across is not a problem. And on the other side is San Sebastian. From there, the terrain is rolling hills all the way to Santiago. I have made the trip many times, and I can tell you that it offers a unique spiritual experience. Isn't that right, Claudine?"

"Yes," came her reply.

Frank tried to fill the vacuum of her terse response: "Yes, I imagine that the *Camino* offers plenty of time and solitude for serious contemplation."

"It is a way to truly meet your deepest self and to strip away the layers of culture and defensiveness, to finally uncover the light of the Christ, who resides within us all," Charles responded.

"You are quite articulate, even eloquent," remarked Millie, attempting to steer the conversation to his writings and their origin. "Do you have any favorite authors or preferred books of the Bible?"

"I suppose you could say that I am partial to the letters of John," he replied. "They express such feeling, such passion for the early church." Millie noticed that Claudine stiffened at his response.

"Any other favorites, for example, from early church fathers or writers during the Reformation?" She was probing further, ready to go as far as he would allow.

Charles then began to list authors, most of whom Millie and Frank remembered from Douglas Parks' list, having multiple 'hits' with the writings of the Apostle John. Millie wondered if he was aware that he was linking himself to these past writers in the chain that went back to the first century. He might not have known of their database and their analysis. But if he did, he was intentionally connecting himself to the entire history of this amazing story. Claudine's body language continued to show discomfort as he spoke.

After lunch, they returned to the SUV, with the light rain retreating to a mist. Millie was extra careful as she navigated the steep meadow to reenter the vehicle. The road led on, upward and further into the mist, which began to enclose the SUV in a fog-like cloud. Relying on Charles' experience with the terrain, Millie and Frank, in the back seat, could no longer see much of anything, including the *Camino* path far below.

Without raising his voice, Charles now calmly commented that they were being followed.

"Last week, I was on this same road and saw headlights behind me. They followed for quite a few kilometers, never coming close enough for me to make out the car or the driver. Then they turned off. Now, I see them again. Do you see them, Claudine?"

"Yes."

Millie wondered about the extent of Claudine's vocabulary.

"Claudine was not with me last week," he went on, causing both Millie and Frank to wonder if she was along today because of the wildlife or because of the stalker. They also wondered if the rifle was standard for her job or if it was called into service because of the following headlights.

They continued on for another thirty minutes, the trailing headlights still keeping their distance. Millie had no knowledge of the likelihood of meeting another vehicle on the path but she assumed that the coincidence was very unusual. The SUV was quiet, as Charles continued to repeatedly glance in his rear-view mirror.

"They are coming up on us." Charles now seemed to be increasingly fixated on the trailing headlights, looking back as much as he looked ahead. From what Millie could see of the road, which by now was little more than a rough path in the fog, they were in a stretch with a steep solid rock embankment on the left, and a sheer drop-off to the right, with the bottom hidden far below. A false move either way would spell disaster.

"Hold on!" He barked, and Claudine pulled her rifle from its casing, tightly gripping it with both hands. Pulling a cartridge magazine from her pouch, she loaded the rifle. The following headlights were now only a few meters behind, and closing in fast.

The SUV sharply accelerated, abruptly pushing the four passengers deep into their seat backs. Millie could only hope that Charles' knowledge of the path would more than compensate for the limited vision afforded him by the fog. He was clearly attempting to outrun the trailing vehicle, avoiding what would no doubt be a dangerous confrontation.

Large rock outcroppings on the left of the SUV now flew past the windows, while the right side showed only the fog-draped abyss. Looking more than a few meters ahead was pointless, as the fog lights were ineffective in the mist. Charles was speeding along, mostly on feel. Millie shivered as she considered the danger, both beside and behind them.

The road offered no opportunity for passing, and no place to pull off and stop. Riding in the back seat felt like a roller-coaster as the SUV traversed dips and rises in the unpaved road, bouncing Millie and Frank so much that they shielded their heads with their hands.

The four passengers could now hear the guttural roar of the following vehicle's engine. Looking back, they could make out a truck with a massive steel cattle guard grille, now inches away from the SUV's rear bumper. The road now entered a stretch of gravel, with small stones uprooted by the SUV's heavy-duty tires flying backward and pelting the truck behind them. It did not slow down, the steel grille easily deflecting the rain of stones off to the side.

Each twist in the road brought new hope that the truck would back off. But it kept pace with the speeding SUV, edging close enough to now and again bump its rear with the massive steel grille. It was impossible to see the driver or to determine if the truck carried any passengers.

For a third time, Charles called out. "Hold on! We're going to make a turn." Millie and Frank were already holding on as best they could, Claudine still gripping her rifle. But it would be impossible for her to shoot from the swerving SUV.

The road now gradually curved to the right, with the rock wall rushing past on one side and the drop-off on the other. Millie couldn't imagine where they could possibly turn. A hard left would plant the SUV squarely on the stone face of the mountain. To the right, and they would plunge through the fog clear to the invisible bottom.

But to her surprise, Charles suddenly jerked the wheel to the left, steering the SUV onto a partially hidden, still-narrower cutoff between two rock faces and off the trail they had been following. The solid rock walls on either side of the SUV were now no more than inches away. Even in the fog they could clearly see the menace of their narrow path, threatening certain destruction of both the vehicle and its passengers with one wrong move.

The following truck vainly tried to follow the SUV's sudden change of direction, but failed to complete the turn. It missed the cutoff, and sped into the solid wall of rock at seventy kph. The horrific crash was audible to the passengers of the SUV even though they were now on the opposite side of the rock face and over a hundred meters away. They could finally stop and catch their breath.

In reverse, the SUV carefully retraced its path, back through the turn-off and to the rock wall where they found the truck, damaged almost beyond recognition and smoldering as if it might at any second explode in flames. The impact had compressed the front end of the truck almost to the firewall.

From the back seat of the SUV, Millie could see the horrific scene: the nearly-destroyed truck, the smoke, and to her horror, she could see, slumped over the steering wheel, a uniformed man, bleeding from his mouth, nose and ears. He was not moving. Alongside him was a second uniformed man, mouth agape, with severe head injuries, also lifeless.

Claudine cautiously walked toward the truck, rifle in hand. She examined the bodies.

"Claudine, are they are dead?" asked Charles.

"Yes," she reported in her clipped manner. She would say no more.

Millie would not normally wish to view such a scene, especially the dead bodies. However, she felt a strange curiosity about these men. In a weird way, she wondered if they might also have been in San Jose weeks before. Were they the killers of Victor Cardenas?

Millie exited the SUV and slowly walked to the still smoldering truck. She peered into the front seat, becoming another eyewitness to the bloody aftermath of the chase.

Millie could now see more: between the men, on the front seat and scattered on the floor, was a small arsenal of weapons, including pistols, rifles and surprisingly, handcuffs.

Charles, now out of the SUV, looked for identification on the bodies. He found none.

As Millie caught her breath, the words of both Dr. Chandler and Sister Camilla spun through her mind. Both of them had expressed so much confidence in her, more than she had in herself, she had to admit. But now, at the scene of a blood-curdling chase, the attempt at a second assassination, and the bodies in the front seat of the truck, she wondered yet again what she was doing here, in the mountains of France, when she might be at home, quietly living out her superficial life.

"Are you okay?" She could dimly hear the words from Charles as if he were speaking through a film of water. "Are you okay? Millie, are you okay?"

"Are you John?" is all that she could think to say.

10

As soon as Millie asked "Are you John?" she wished that she could take it back.

But it was out. It was out, and it could not be taken back. Millie's question hung in the air for a long moment. It had found its way out of her mouth, quite by accident, hurried through her consciousness and passed through her lips, triggered by the emotion of the last forty-five minutes. She did not mean to ask this question, not now anyway, and not without much more evidence. But there it was, almost floating, practically visible in the misty air, unmistakable. The eyes of Frank, Charles and Claudine now turned to her.

Then Charles: "Am I John? John who? If you tell me who *you* really are, then I might answer such a question."

Neither Frank nor Millie could recover in any way other than to tell the truth.

"Let me catch my breath. Then let's go back to the center and we will have a talk," she responded. "You are correct, in the sense that we are here for a reason different from what we've told you. But please know that we are not here to harm you or anyone."

"Yes, let me also assure you," added Frank, "that we are not here for any malicious reason. But you have a right to know why we're here and we will speak openly."

They got back into the SUV and rode in silence back to the Naissance Center. After changing into dry clothes, they walked to the social center, which was almost empty. Sitting in front of a fireplace, they waited for Millie to speak. She knew that it was up to her to reveal their purpose, without sharing any more than necessary. She thought of Douglas Parks' emphasis on confidentiality. But her native honesty prevailed over any thought of cloaking what had to be openly said.

"Frank and I are here on a mission," she began, "that has nothing to do with Santiago de Compostela. I apologize for the deception. We have been given your name, Charles, because of your writings. You see, your writing style has been found to be identical to that of a certain figure from the Bible. Over the centuries, quite a few individuals have written in this same style, suggesting that," and she paused to take a deep breath, "that this figure from the Bible may still be alive, as strange as that sounds. Your writings, Charles, suggest that you may be one of those individuals. Actually, we are quite sure that you are, in fact, one of those individuals."

"But it's only a theory," interjected Frank, "although backed up by significant computer analysis. Your writings have perfectly matched those of this first century Biblical figure. We have been sent here to find out if you, are in fact, in some form, or in some way, connected to this Biblical figure."

There was a pause; an awkward pause, as if each of them was waiting for someone else to speak.

"Who sent you?" Charles was not going to reveal anything until more questions were answered. "And do you have any connection to the two men in the truck?"

"A foundation has organized a research team," answered Frank, "and we are members of that team. We cannot reveal the identity of the foundation. Even we do not know who it is. But I can tell you that we trust those who called us into this, and our purpose is not to do harm to anyone. We have no idea of the identity of the men in the truck."

"But I must tell you," Millie went on, "that though we don't know who those men were, we do fear that you may be in danger. Those men may have also known about your writings and your connection to the figure from the Bible. I have already met one such individual like yourself who was killed and I do not wish the same result for you. You need to be aware that others besides ourselves, others with evil intent, are searching for you. That is, assuming that you are who we think you are."

"You called me John, didn't you?" Charles asked. "John who? Who do you say that I am?"

Here it was, the point where Millie and Frank must play all of their cards. Millie had no choice but to answer in as direct a way as possible.

"We think that you are the Apostle John, called St. John the Divine, the Beloved Disciple, the witness to the Christ, the writer of the Gospel of John, the letters of John, and possibly, the Revelation to John. Somehow, still living after two thousand years."

There was little else that she could add; it was as clear as she could make it. And sounding as far-fetched, she was thinking.

Charles and Claudine traded glances. Now it was their turn.

"I am not obligated to tell you anything at all, do you understand that? Do you understand that?" His opening was not what they wanted to hear. "I do not know how you found me or what analysis led you to me. I have wondered if this day might come, but I am prepared for it. For this is why I am who I am."

His opening remarks gave them nothing but confusion. Hopefully, he would go on.

And he did. "I am not the Apostle John." He repeated, "I am not the Apostle John."

Thinking that he was finished, Millie broke in, "But your writings, all of them, match the writings of the Apostle John. How do you explain that?"

"Let me finish," he replied. "It is true, I am not the Apostle John. But it is also true that I have been called, and I have been gifted, to serve our Lord in a way that protects the true Apostle John. You see, I am a decoy, a stand-in, called to distract any agent of evil who would search for John to do him harm. Do you understand?"

Millie hoped that he would go on, and he did.

"This calling, the one I have been given, is a great honor. And if need be, I am ready to sacrifice my life in the service of the one who called me, no one less than the Christ himself. There is no greater love than this, to lay down one's life for a friend. And as he laid down his life for me, I am prepared to lay mine down for him, if I can protect the true Apostle John."

"And Claudine," Frank asked, "what about her?"

"I have been called to appear to be the Apostle John," Charles began, "to deceive forces of evil who have sought his life for two thousand years. I am one of a long line of decoys, happy to be called to this service. Claudine is a gift to me from our Lord, a protector. She will, if need be, sacrifice her life to make my role more believable, and to safeguard me from forces like those we saw today. Isn't that right, Claudine?"

"Yes."

"Then we must warn you," began Millie, "that we have already seen another one of your same calling brutally murdered. Those men today clearly had the same intent. Others will follow. I fear that we have brought this on you."

"You mustn't worry," replied Charles. "First of all, we are prepared for these attempts. Claudine and I are very resourceful. Just as we repelled the attempt today, we are ready to repel them all. But even if the next attempt succeeds, we will have served our purpose. We are prepared to die for our calling. Do you understand?"

"But how do we know," asked Frank, "that you are truly a decoy and not the Apostle John? How can we know? After all, you could be the Apostle John and you could be using the story you just gave us to throw us off. What do you say?"

"I do not say any more than I have said," responded Charles. "You do not know for sure and you will never know. My calling is from above. My style of writing is a gift from above. The human mind will not be able to resolve this. You have no choice but to believe me. In fact, the only way to know for sure is to kill me to see if the Risen Christ returns."

He went on. "I did not ask for this gift. This was a calling, not an invitation that I could decline."

He now seemed different, not the relaxed, carefree young man Charles, the hiker and counselor at the Naissance Center, but someone older, more complex, and more formidable. Was this the real Charles? Or was it John?

He continued, "But I welcome it. Even I do not understand how this came to be, how I was chosen and how my words match so clearly those of the Apostle John. For a time I wrestled with this calling and even tried to reject it. I could not. And now I embrace it and delight, in fact, in my lack of understanding. It is purely a matter of faith. I cannot see but I believe.

"And now," he went on, "you two have a choice. You may believe me or you may not. You may report back to your mysterious foundation that you have found John, or you may report yet another detour designed by none other than the Holy Spirit, meant to camouflage the true John and stymie those who wish to kill him. The true John. A hidden figure. A figure who is beyond my knowing. A figure who has been in the shadows for two thousand years. Or perhaps -- a figure who is in plain sight but who is unrecognizable."

Millie: "Thank you, Charles. Thank you, Claudine. We will leave to-morrow. Our quest is not over, but we need bother you no longer."

"We will pray for your safety," went on Frank. "You are blessed of God." And it was over.

Millie noticed a voice mail on her phone as she was packing that night for departure the following morning. *Probably Randall*, she thought, as she started to listen.

But then she noticed the phone number, one that she did not recognize. Listening to the message, she realized that it was Douglas Parks, violating his own rules of confidentiality.

"Millie, the message began, "I want you and Frank to make a detour before returning home. Just across the Pyrenees, in northern Spain, is an estate, a *hacienda*, which I want you to visit. When you arrive, you will be told what to do. I have sent the directions to Frank to avoid putting too much into one message. I hope this is clear enough. Good bye."

Combining her message with Frank's showed a drive of several hours across the Pyrenees, into northern Spain, a lightly-populated area noted for its wine production. Neither Millie nor Frank could imagine why this detour was assigned to them, but both assumed that it was important if Parks had chosen to violate his policy on private communications.

Early the next morning, Charles and Claudine met them to say good-bye. It seemed to Millie quite different from her parting with Father Cardenas and Juan, back in San Jose. She had not become emotionally close to either one of these individuals, though she greatly admired both of them. And she genuinely feared for their safety.

"We hope you have a safe journey home," said Charles, not knowing about their extended trip. "Don't we, Claudine?"

"Yes," she replied, with as much emotion as she could muster.

As they began to drive away, Charles held up his hand to stop them. "I almost forgot," he said. "Apparently another one of your team is coming to see us here. I might have thought we had talked you out of the notion that I am the person you are looking for."

"Who is it?" asked Millie.

"Two people, actually," he replied. "Do you know Marianne Weems and Hans Oltorf? They plan to arrive tomorrow. Do you know why they are coming?"

"Yes, we do know them and no, we didn't know about their visit here," replied Millie, "and I advise you not to meet with them until you hear further from Frank and me." This turn of events confirmed Millie's apprehension regarding Marianne. She immediately phoned Douglas Parks.

"Why are you phoning me?" was his initial reaction to her call. "I gave you and Frank all the instructions you will need for your trip to Spain. My call was an exception and I insist that we continue to avoid unprotected communications."

Without bothering to explain, Millie asked, "Douglas, have you sent Marianne Weems and Hans Oltorf to follow us to France?"

"No, of course not. Why do you ask?"

"They are scheduled to arrive here tomorrow. What should we do?"

There was a pause as Parks thought it through. "Certainly, you need to warn Charles Boutte. On second thought, I will warn him myself, not to meet with them, and to protect himself as he finds necessary. We have no idea of their purpose in following you to France, isn't that right?"

"I believe I do know," commented Millie wryly.

11

Neither Millie nor Frank had any idea why Douglas Parks had diverted them to Spain. As they drove, they considered every possibility that they could imagine. The most likely was that they were being sent to interview a new candidate who had recently been discovered in the software. But that, they admitted to themselves, was only a guess.

The drive across the Pyrenees into Spain was scenic, following winding mountain roads, passing through small villages, as remote as Millie had ever seen. Aside from the mountains, it reminded her a bit of the mostly empty countryside around Plostina, in central Texas. It felt like the end of the world, with mile after mile of quiet mountain meadows, and snow cleared to the sides of the road in the higher altitudes. As they left France, they entered the eastern border of the Principality of Andorra, whose common language is Catalan, and whose origin dates to the tenth century.

Stopping for lunch in a local Andorran café, Millie and Frank were surprised to see dozens of pig legs hanging on wire, from wall to wall. They learned that these are a delicacy of the Pyrenees, prepared by locals using smoking huts high up in the dry air of the mountains. Upon their request, the waiter unhooked one from its wire and delivered several slices to their table, returning the remainder to its hook. It was a bit macabre, but quite delicious.

As they entered Spain, Millie's thoughts returned to the *Camino de Santiago*, the pilgrimage that had been their entre to Charles Boutte. It was clearly not the tourist attraction that she'd first imagined. Instead, the *Camino* offered an opportunity for a deep spiritual experience -- one that she, surprisingly, found herself hungry to taste. Perhaps, after this side trip to the *hacienda*, she might tack on a stint on the *Camino*, assuming, of course, that she could navigate the path without too much difficulty.

Parks' directions took them on, following primitive "C" level roads into the rolling hills of northern Spain. Their final destination, the *hacienda*, was over twenty kilometers from the nearest village. Its gate was open, and they entered, following a narrow drive that went for about one kilometer. Millie could see cattle grazing in a distant pasture. It was obvious that someone very wealthy lived here.

Millie and Frank had no idea what to expect in light of Parks' typically scant instructions. It seemed that for him, everything must be taken on faith. He could never be accused of over-communicating. And there was no reason to even speculate on how this detour might have any possible connection to their mission.

The *hacienda* was expansive, with a high brick wall, at the center of which was an elaborate iron gate anchored by a wooden door with iron hinges and ornate hardware. They parked on the gravel driveway and peered inside the gate to see a courtyard, complete with bubbling fountain. The house itself was stucco, two stories with wooden shutters on the windows, mostly closed in the chill air. Smoke billowed from several fireplaces which jutted from the tiled roof.

They had been noticed. As they approached the house, its massive wooden front door opened, revealing a smallish man in his sixties, his white hair groomed to perfection, wearing slacks, a sweater tied around his neck, and Italian-made loafers. He greeted them pleasantly.

"*Bienvenidos!* Welcome, I am so happy to greet you. You are, of course, Millie and Monsignor Morelli. I am Enrique Cardenas, and this is the Cardenas estate."

After exchanging additional greetings, they followed Enrique inside the main entry hall, servants retrieving their bags from the car and taking them to bedrooms upstairs. Enrique motioned Millie and Frank into a study and to a sofa close to one of the fireplaces, which was putting out a cozy warmth that was welcome in the chill of the late afternoon. A tray was already in front of them, loaded with pastries, fruit and *jamon*. Coffee was steaming in a silver service.

"We have been expecting you. I hope that you will stay with us for at least a few days," began Enrique. "We have much to cover with you, hopefully to make things clear."

That would be refreshing, thought Millie, though it would have been politically incorrect to say so. "All we know is that we've been sent here without knowing why," she said in her sweetest voice.

"Yes, of course," Enrique replied. "And I will not waste time with a lot of pleasantries without coming to the point. I do hope that your stay will include pleasantries, of course, but there will be time for them later. For now, let me explain that I am aware of your mission and have been in contact with Douglas Parks and Dr. Chandler. They have briefed me on your activities and have asked for my help.

"In fact," he went on, "I am allied with the foundation that organized your project from the beginning. You see, my family has had a history with, shall we say, protecting a certain party from forces who might wish to do him harm. And when I say history, I mean a long history, over many centuries. This estate, for example, has been in my family for over six hundred years. And we have other estates, *fincas* I believe they call them, in the New World."

The light bulb immediately went on for Millie, though not yet for Frank.

"This must be more than coincidental. Then, Senor Cardenas, are you possibly related to Father Victor Cardenas in Guatemala?"

"Victor Cardenas, God rest his soul, was my cousin. You see, our family owns the *finca* at San Jose, in Guatemala. It was granted to us by the Spanish crown in the sixteenth century. Its priests have typically been members of the Cardenas family. Victor was the latest in a long line of them, going back to the beginning of Antigua and New Spain. Victor actually grew up on this estate before entering the priesthood.

"And I am aware," he went on, "that you, Millie, were in San Jose just before Victor was murdered. It must have been terribly shocking when you heard the news. And I am sure that by now, you understand that Victor was a *senuelo*, a decoy for the Apostle John. It was the privilege of his life to do so and you should know that he gave his life gladly to protect John from the forces who seek to kill him."

Millie wasn't sure if this news should make her feel relieved that the Apostle John hadn't been killed, or if she should feel even more grieved at the sacrifice of Father Cardenas.

"By the way," Enrique went on, "we have brought Victor's remains back here, to the estate, to be interred in the family cemetery. You may visit it, if you like, while you are here."

"Yes," she replied, "I would very much like to do so. I became very fond of Father Cardenas during my short stay in Antigua." And the memories of Father Cardenas and her stay in Antigua returned to flood Millie's mind, bringing back her feelings of sorrow over the death of the courageous priest.

"Let us now go further into the murder of my cousin," Cardenas went on. "Tell me what you know and what you think about the killers."

"There is much to tell you." Millie knew that she must steel herself to remember Father Cardenas with as little emotion over his murder as she could. "We can also update you on our recent experience in France. It is all beginning to fit together and I find it very troubling."

"Yes, of course. I am aware of Charles Boutte at the Naissance Center. I actually helped to identify him as a candidate to serve as a decoy."

"While we were visiting him, he was the target of an assassination attempt," reported Frank. We all barely escaped two men who were intent on killing him. We were just along for the ride, together with Claudine, his associate."

"We must wonder," added Millie, "if these men were connected to the assassins in San Jose."

"Yes, I know about the attempt. The two in France also participated in the assassination of my cousin," reported Enrique. "We know who they were and we know who they represented."

"Is this some kind of network, or some sinister organization?" asked Millie.

"I believe Monsignor Morelli knows the answer to that question," Enrique replied, without looking up. Millie turned to Frank with a surprised look on her face.

"Frank?" Millie was amazed by what she heard.

"I'm not exactly who you were told I was, Millie," began Frank. "Douglas Parks told you that I am an archivist at the Vatican. That is not exactly true. I do work at the Vatican but I'm not an archivist. In fact, I'm associated with a security group that researches and investigates organizations that seek to spread evil across the world, especially violence against Christians.

"My present assignment is this project. We learned some time ago that a certain organization was actively attempting to penetrate the walls of security that have for two thousand years protected the Apostle John."

"And what have you found, Monsignor? Can you tell us?" asked Enrique. Millie suspected that he already knew the answer to this question.

"There is an association, a loose network if you will. *La Noche de Oscuridad.* The Night of Darkness. Branches of this organization exist across Europe, especially in Eastern Europe. Unlike many satanic cults, this organization has an avowed purpose of evil. It actively seeks to do harm."

"Has it existed for long?" Millie had never heard of it.

"These organizations seem to shed their skin every few years and morph from one into another. Mostly they live only as long as their charismatic leader. Once he or she is gone, they seem to either go into hibernation or merge into another group. *La Noche* is different: it has existed since at least the end of World War II, surviving through several generations of leadership. But its roots can be traced all the way back to medieval times."

Frank went on: "This particular organization seems to be obsessed with finding and killing the Apostle John. All attempts thus far have proven unsuccessful, though innocent people have lost their lives in the process."

"Like Father Cardenas," added Millie. "And I almost forgot, what about Juan? He was almost killed in the assassination. What happened to him? He was such a sweet old man. He seems to have disappeared."

"Juan survived," commented Enrique, adding no further explanation.

"So why are we here, Senor Cardenas?" Millie still sensed that there was something yet unsaid.

"First of all, please call me Enrique. And second, you are here to brief me on your activities and also on your thoughts about where we go from here. It is clear that the project's security has been breached. Your two associates, Marianne Weems and Hans Oltorf, appeared at the Naissance Center, against the strict orders of Douglas Parks. As far as we know, they are still there. What are your thoughts?"

Millie was quick to respond. "I believe that Charles and Claudine are in danger. Hans Oltorf is a stranger to me but I traveled with Marianne Weems to Guatemala and found her to be, shall we say, unpredictable. Maybe it's just instinct but she seemed to have an agenda different from what we were instructed. If those two have taken it upon themselves to visit Charles without direction from Douglas Parks, it can mean nothing but trouble -- in my opinion. And further, I believe that the attack on the mountain road must have been orchestrated by them. Okay, *might* have been orchestrated by them." She didn't want to sound too certain. But in her own mind, she was certain.

"Millie, I can now see why Dr. Chandler was so eager for you to join this project," Enrique commented in his gracious manner. "I value your observations and also your candor. Your judgment is to be trusted. I appreciate that you speak your mind and that you do so in a non-threatening manner.

"But now, we have discussed enough for the present. I promised you some pleasantries, to make your stay enjoyable. So let me give you a tour of the *Hacienda de Cardenas.*"

"I would love a tour," began Millie, "and especially to see where Father Cardenas is buried. And if you have any further information on Juan, I would love to hear it. He was so gracious and also such an effective protector of Father Cardenas; I know he must have been so terribly upset at

Father Cardenas' assassination. I am certain, though, that he could have done nothing to stop it."

"Yes," responded Enrique, "there was nothing that Juan could do. And yes, he was terribly upset and he blamed himself. We have all tried to console him and to remind him that he did all he could, that Victor knew that this day might come. He was prepared for it. And Victor never doubted his purpose."

"Well," remarked Millie, "if you do have any further news about Juan, please let me know. I became very fond of both of them during our stay in Antigua."

"Yes," responded Enrique, "I certainly will."

12

The tour of the Cardenas estate was impressive to say the least. Millie's childhood in a small ranching community in central Texas did not prepare her for the opulence that she saw at the *hacienda*. The stables were luxurious (*I could live in one of these stalls*, she thought to herself), and the horse ring was beyond anything she'd seen. There was even a small vineyard growing Tempranillo grapes. At harvest, these were sent to a local processing cooperative to be made into a wonderful private label *crianza* and an even more special *reserva* that would accompany their meals.

Enrique drove Millie and Frank over the estate in a pristine four-wheeler that had clearly never gone off-road. His pastures were carpeted with a rich turf, which as Enrique explained, was especially suited to the local Asturian Mountain breed of cattle.

Everything had seemingly been carefully thought out and all was much more than first class.

And yet the estate, with all its impressive wealth, was not intimidating to Millie. Instead, she felt a warmth, not only from the estate, but also from Enrique himself, the same warmth that she had felt from his cousin Victor, far away in Guatemala. In a way, it felt home-like to her, as if she were a welcome long-lost relative.

Their last stop was the estate's cemetery, where centuries of Cardenas family members were resting. A small mausoleum was at its center, and as Enrique explained, it housed the earliest generations of the family. The newest grave, closer to the gate, belonged to Father Victor Cardenas, with whom Millie felt a tender bond.

"I had no brothers. Victor was a brother to me. He loved this estate," Enrique explained. "He entered the priesthood and went to Guatemala only as a matter of family duty. I believe he eventually came to also love San Jose, but always, he longed to return here. I am sorry that he did so in this manner, before he could retire and spend his later years here as a gentleman rancher."

Millie's eyes filled with tears. She would always remember Father Cardenas, tending the lonely outpost church in San Jose, eating his meager meals with Juan, lamenting his snub from Rome -- all because he stood in unity with the poor.

Enrique went on, as if reading Millie's mind. "Victor was never afraid to take up a cause. The poor of Guatemala were his mission and his ministry. He would never forsake them -- and he paid the price for it. He would always say, 'these are my friends, my brothers and my sisters. If my life ever amounts to anything, it will be because I have embraced them.'"

And in a solitary reflection, "I was fortunate. Victor was older, and by the time I came of age, he had already entered the priesthood. And he was quickly identified as a decoy for John." Enrique softly chuckled, almost to himself, "And you know, I would not have made a very good priest.

"So, I stayed here, on this estate, tending the family's cattle and growing things. Our Lord, however, had other plans, though I could not see them coming. And they began with the shock of great suffering. Suffering that I could neither explain nor justify. My anger at God raged for years. I just could not see why these things had to happen.

"Even in the midst of my anger, though, our Lord did not desert me. He surrounded me with love and support, which I failed to appreciate for a long time. Finally, I did. I was able to look back and see His hand -- to see His hand in everything.

"And yes, at long last, I could begin to see, as our friend the Apostle Paul says, 'through a glass, darkly.' New causes tugged at me. The larger world presented itself, in all its beauty and all its danger. This estate and this valley began to smother me and I needed to live on a larger stage. That is why we are talking today, because I have chosen a larger stage. But I too, like Victor, paid a price. We must all be prepared to suffer. We do, at least, if we are people of faith.

"I don't know why I've become so philosophical all of a sudden. Please excuse me."

Millie could now see in Enrique, more than a physical resemblance to Father Cardenas. She could see a heart that yearned for something more. Like Victor, Enrique had been called to serve, to reach out, even to fight a power structure that in its own way, had produced the very wealth that fueled his calling. And she could also see a deep pain.

Before leaving the cemetery, Enrique stopped at a cluster of graves near Victor's beside the gate. Standing in silence alongside Enrique, Millie contemplated the story that must have produced these memorials. In the center was Maria, clearly Enrique's late wife. She was surrounded by three smaller monuments, to Carlos, Imelda and Victor. The markers showed the same date of death for all four. The story for these would need to wait until later.

After a sumptuous dinner, they retired to Enrique's study. Cigars would have been customary but Enrique deferred to Millie's preference. Outwardly, she seemed fragile to him. He'd noticed her difficulty walking, though she'd not worn her braces. And now at the end of a tiring day, he could see her hands trembling as she lifted a glass of port.

"Are you all right?"

"Yes, of course. But I do have some physical issues. They are not a problem. Only when I get really tired."

"Yes, I have noticed." He went on, "I do not imagine such physical problems can slow you down, Millie. You demonstrate a serious determination. It will be interesting to see what your present quest will demand of you."

"Enrique, it has already demanded more than I thought I could give. And I know that more surprises await me. But I must say that the joy of getting to know people like Father Cardenas, Juan, Charles Boutte and yourself has gone way beyond my imagining. And you too, of course,

Frank. I guess I've learned that my life was missing deeper relationships with a spiritual foundation. Since childhood, I have not really had that." Her words brought back memories of Father Vlacek. *That dangling thread is surely being pulled now*, she thought to herself.

Frank raised a question that Millie had also pondered: "We were told that one of the targets of our analysis, the English banker, had a history of writings that included some that matched the Apostle John and some that did not. Enrique, how can that happen?"

"It is part of the plan. We hope to confuse the enemy," Enrique responded. Millie was surprised that he was so conversant about the entire program. "You see, we needed to plant the idea that our results were not consistent and somewhat inconclusive. The banker's results demonstrate that, and in so doing, we hope to plant doubt about the reliability of our software programs. If they cannot be relied upon one hundred percent, then the enemy will need to resort to a much slower process of physical analysis and interpretation."

Before retiring for the night, Millie phoned home. It had been over a week since she'd spoken to Randall and he needed to know that she was all right.

"I know that you can't tell me where you are," he began, "but you can at least tell me that you're okay. I do care about you, whether you believe that or not."

"Yes, I'm fine." She was sure that telling him about her near-death experience in France was not the thing to do. It was hard to determine what she could share, and consequently, she decided to share nothing.

So they proceeded with some small talk about Paul and Leslie, both of whom were fine. The topic of their marriage and Randall's infidelities did not come up.

Just as they were saying good-bye, Randall remembered: "Oh yes, I almost forgot; about a week ago you received several calls from someone who works with you on your project. I believe her name is Weems, Marianne Weems, and she seemed pretty insistent on finding out where you are."

Just as Millie was about to say "Don't dare tell her anything," he added, "Of course, since I don't know where you are, I couldn't tell her. If she calls again, what would you like for me to say?"

Millie tried to avoid sounding alarmed but it was useless. "Tell her that I will be home soon and that we'll talk then."

"Okay," he replied slowly. "But is that really true? Will you, in fact, be home soon? You sound weird. Are you sure you're all right?"

"Yes, now I have to go. I'll phone again soon."

The next morning, over a hearty *hacienda* breakfast, Enrique brought news from Charles. He and Claudine had successfully avoided Marianne Weems and Hans Oltorf. They had intentionally been away when the pair arrived. And when Marianne and Hans returned, they were away again. The visitors had then left, or at least it appeared that they had left.

Millie knew that they would not give up so easily. Charles and Claudine knew to be on their guard.

"What else can I tell you?" asked Enrique.

"I have so many questions," Millie began, "and not to criticize Douglas Parks, but he told us so little. For example, how many decoys are there?"

"I do not know," responded Enrique. "It would be dangerous to know that. You see, if our enemy knew, they could narrow down the numbers by killing decoys until there were just one or two left. And then they would know that they had their man. So, it would be beneficial if they thought there were hundreds, even thousands, although we must assume that it is a much smaller number. I am not sure that anyone knows the answer to your question, and it's better for everyone if that is the case."

Millie thought to herself that *La Noche* seemed to be doing just what Enrique thought they would not: killing candidates, one by one, until there was only one left. Only after they had killed the final candidate, she reasoned, could they be sure that one of them had truly been the Apostle John, even if they didn't know exactly which one. Killing them all would be the only way they could be certain. And then, if Christ did not return, they would go public with the fact that John was dead and Jesus' prophecy was false. As a result, the faith of millions would be weakened.

Frank: "Is there some kind of communications network that links all the members of this protection group? I mean, does one decoy know who the other decoys are? Can they communicate? Is there a central command center, with authority to make decisions and to identify new decoys?"

"All good questions, and not surprising from a Roman Catholic priest," answered Enrique. "And please believe me when I tell you that I do not know, I really do not know. Nor do I wish to know. And I'm not aware of anyone else who does know. You must understand that it is better this way, that there is no command center that controls everything, that could itself become a target. All is hidden. All is organic in the sense that there is no organization chart, no hierarchy of officials. This is not a corporation and it is certainly not the Roman Catholic Church!"

"Well, surely you can answer this question, Enrique," began Millie. "Where do we go from here? What do we do next? How do we deal with Marianne Weems and Hans Oltorf?"

"Yes, those are very good questions," he replied. "We must assume, mustn't we, that Marianne Weems and Hans Oltorf are in the enemy's camp, and have infiltrated our project. How unfortunate. If I know the *La Noche* organization, they will not give up easily. This chase has been going on for two thousand years and I have no reason to believe that it will end until our Blessed Lord returns and the Apostle John's long wait is over.

"We must find out where Weems and Oltorf are. The other candidates, wherever they are, must be notified to take extreme care. Weems and Oltorf must be cut out of all communications."

"Is it realistic to think that perhaps we should eliminate Weems and Oltorf?" asked Frank. "Shouldn't we take the initiative or must we simply wait for them to act and hope that we can react?"

"All I know," answered Enrique, "is that we must find Weems and Oltorf, isolate them and render them useless to their cause. We must also believe that they are not the leaders, the planners of their organization. It is more likely that they are simply 'soldiers' recruited to carry out the plans of someone higher up."

Millie's head was spinning. There was so much uncertainty, and so many questions that had no answers. She felt called to pray and found herself in the cemetery, kneeling before the grave of Father Cardenas.

"Father God, I am so confused, so torn, so uncertain. Yet I know that I am your servant and you call me to love you and to love my neighbor, no matter what. I know that you also call me to obey, even when the path is not clear or if there is danger ahead. You have brought me so far, so far from Plostina, from my home, from my deep sleep, and I am so grateful that you have called me into your light. I thank you for surrounding me with saints who witness to you with their very lives. And I feel so inadequate compared to them. Lord, strengthen me. Let your Spirit that lives within me find the path that you would have me follow. And Lord, please continue to place angels on my path as you have done. In the Holy Name of Christ I pray, amen."

With tears in her eyes, she remained, kneeling at the grave of Father Cardenas. Her legs ached from the strain, but still she remained. Finally, she felt a release to rise and when she did, she saw a figure, an old man, just now leaving the cemetery. She had not noticed him before.

And as he turned back, her eyes astonished her with what they saw. "Juan?"

13

Juan, the sexton from the church in San Jose, was now in Spain, still recuperating from the wounds he received in the assassination of Father Cardenas.

"It is so good to see you again, my child," he began. "I have wondered what became of you, and I have prayed for your safety. And what a miracle it is for us to meet here, especially, a world away from Guatemala!"

The emotion of the moment overcame Millie and she began to sob. "I don't know what is making me cry like this," she tried to explain, "but seeing you here is such a demonstration of God's blessings, and such a joyful surprise. I have worried about you, Juan, but now, I'm so delighted to see you, and so sorry if my tears make me appear sad."

"They do not, my child, as all who love our Lord must learn. Tears can be the greatest witness to the one who is our shepherd in all things. Just as sometimes laughter can also be a wonderful witness to the Advocate, the Spirit who lives within us."

"How long have you been here?" She wanted to ask him so many questions.

"I accompanied the remains of Father Cardenas here, soon after his death. The Guatemalan authorities detained me for a time, questioning me, but they finally allowed me to come here. I have been very well cared for here, you must know. But now, if you will excuse me, we are late;

shall we attend Mass?" And he gestured to a small, nondescript chapel, adjacent to the cemetery. Millie had barely noticed it during the previous day's tour, thinking it was just another outbuilding. Nor had Enrique mentioned it.

They entered the small chapel. Its architecture looked quite primitive compared to the other buildings on the estate. The interior was all stone, with an unpolished stone floor and a slate roof. Several crypts hugged the walls, which had no decorations of any kind. Windows were open air, with no glass. They were tiny, allowing only a small amount of light to enter. A simple cross adorned the stone altar. Iron candle stands stood on either side, accounting for most of the light in the chapel. Millie shuddered as she remembered that it was an iron candle stand that gave Juan his serious head wounds.

Enrique was already present, sitting at the front with Frank, who would celebrate the Mass. He rose and asked if anyone wished to open in prayer.

Juan: "Please allow me the privilege to pray." And he began, "Father, we come to you as a people in darkness, seeking your light, the light that illumines all of the world. We come as your children, as your sheep needing a shepherd, the Good Shepherd. We come seeking the fullness of your blessing, and we thank you and praise you for the truth that you are the one, the light of the world. You truly are the vine and we are the branches. We ask your blessing on our visitors here today, and praise you for the fruit that they bear. Keep them safe, Lord, and let them continue to live in your light, the light that overcomes all darkness. Amen."

Frank, dressed in his ordinary clothes, celebrated the Mass. "My ecclesiastical robes are back in the States," he explained. "In a way, perhaps this is more fitting here in the chapel, since it is so simple with nothing ornate to decorate it."

After the final blessing, Enrique explained, "The chapel pre-dates the estate, going back to the ninth century. It was built by the first Christians in this area. We do not know who they were, nor do we know who is in the crypts. We've never opened them. The carved stone inscriptions on them have long since faded, literally eroding from the elements over the centuries. Since the estate was established in the sixteenth century, nothing has been done to update or modernize this chapel. It is just as it was."

Juan did not join them for coffee after Mass. Millie would have liked to spend hours with him, learning more of his past and of Father Cardenas. That would have to wait.

"We have no new intelligence on the two who tried to visit Charles Boutte," Enrique began. "That is troubling, as we do not know if they will try again or if they will shift their focus to other candidates. Nor do we know if there are others searching for John. I have asked Douglas Parks to retrace his steps in recruiting Weems and Oltorf, to see if he can learn anything, where he went wrong."

Millie related her conversation with Randall from the previous evening. "They certainly seem to be aggressively searching," she concluded, "and it seems that they are not afraid of alerting Douglas Parks and Dr. Chandler."

"I believe the term for that," added Frank, "is that they have gone 'rogue' on us, and no longer pretend to be part of our team. That means that they are in a hurry and perhaps believe that they are close to their objective, to find and kill the Apostle John.

"If Parks and Dr. Chandler knew of other John candidates, they didn't tell us," continued Frank. "However, they did tell us that the software program was going to analyze more texts and that it might be possible to uncover others. We can only hope that if they did, they've tightened the security enough to prevent any further access from our two interlopers."

"Yes," added Millie, "and it's disturbing to think, as I recall, that Marianne was one of the developers of the software. If she worked on the security in the software, she might easily be able to penetrate it and view the entire database. That would mean that she could theoretically find all of the John candidates before we can."

"We must act," Enrique asserted with a tone of authority. "We cannot simply wait until these agents of evil surface again. We have no choice, in my opinion, but to enlist Douglas Parks and Dr. Chandler to meet with us to develop a plan to throw them off their search."

"Yes," agreed Frank, "and remember that there is one other person on our team, who we briefly met, Hugh Matthews, the English Shakespearean professor. We'll need to bring him into this as well."

Meanwhile, a hundred kilometers to the north in France, Charles and Claudine were deliberating their next steps. Following the failed attempt on the mountain road, Marianne Weems and Hans Oltorf had arrived, twice asking for Charles Boutte at the Naissance Center. Center personnel had told them that Charles was in Toulouse for at least several days, with an indeterminate return. As far as Charles knew, Claudine was not known to them. Hopefully, that would be an asset.

In fact, Charles and Claudine were holed up in one of the Center's mountain huts, available for emergencies in case of sudden snowstorms during hiking or skiing activities. Even the Center personnel didn't know their whereabouts.

Clearly, they couldn't stay in the hut for any long period of time and would need to re-surface at some point. Assuming the two attackers did not get discouraged and leave, they would eventually have to face them, hopefully on favorable terms.

They finally decided that the best course of action was to confront Weems and Oltorf in the mountains, and to surprise them with the unexpected presence of Claudine.

Charles phoned the Center's reception office to request that any future inquiries from Weems and Oltorf should be routed to him on his cell phone. He would take it from there. After two days of waiting, his phone rang.

"Hello, this is Charles Boutte," he began. "Who is this?"

"I am a reporter from an American magazine, looking to do a story on the Naissance Center," came the female voice at the other end. "We'd like to interview you for our story, if you can make yourself available."

"Yes, of course," he replied, "That would be splendid, to get some publicity for our center in the American media. I will place myself at your disposal. The only thing is that I am temporarily working to repair one of our mountain huts, so you will need to come up here to interview me. If I give you directions, can you do that?"

"Yes, of course. The directions, please."

The following morning, as planned, the four-wheel-drive jeep carrying Marianne Weems and Hans Oltorf neared the mountain hut. Charles was alone inside, waiting. The jeep parked a hundred meters from the hut, Marianne walking directly toward the front door, and Hans trailing behind, heading toward the side of the hut. He was hoping to find a window through which he might fire a shot. However, finding none, nor a back door, he simply waited in the trees that circled the hut while Marianne went inside.

She did not bother to knock. Entering, she greeted Charles politely. "This shouldn't take long," she said as he gestured for her to sit down. It was clear that there would be no pleasantries in this visit and he did not offer her any refreshment.

"I am glad that you were able to find me here in this remote place. Hopefully it was not an inconvenience to come up here."

"Not in the least. I have wanted to meet you for some time," she replied. "And the location is actually preferable, as I can get you alone here in the mountains. You are a person of some note, mostly from your writings, which are widely known."

"You are too kind," he replied, waiting for her to initiate whatever approach she had planned.

But she wanted, it seemed, to make sure that she had the right man. "You are, are you not, Charles Boutte, the author of a number of books and articles, and the blogger who is so popular?"

"Yes, of course," he replied, "but you are here to learn about the Naissance Center. My writings should be of little interest to you and your readers."

"On the contrary, I find your writings very interesting," she replied, "and I have to tell you that your writings are linked to those of another author from antiquity. Are you aware of that?"

"Yes, I have heard that there is a similarity, a resemblance to the writings of others over the centuries. Frankly, I have no explanation for that," he went on.

"Then you are clearly the person I have been looking for, and your name is not really Charles Boutte, isn't that correct?"

"I don't know what you mean," he replied, and the room grew tense as she began to narrow down on his supposed identity. He played along as best he could. Each believed they held the cards in this exchange.

"Then I must tell you," her voice rising as her pulse raced, "that your writings are now over, and that your death will prove the fallacy of a prophecy that should never have been made and which will never again be believed!

"Hans! Now!" Marianne had not noticed the absence of windows until just then. But nonetheless, Hans was ready, bursting through the door with his pistol cocked and ready.

"We have looked for you for many centuries," Marianne began, "and now that we have found you, we are going to take our time. You must understand that the pleasure we derive from this will be in proportion to the frustration of our long search. It would be a mistake to end this too quickly. Hans, tie him up!"

Hans produced a cord from his backpack and under the authority of his pistol, had Charles sit in a chair with a back that could be used for the loops of the cord. Charles did not resist. Hans tightly tied him to the chair, smiling as he worked, while Marianne held the pistol.

"We're going to take a few pictures, if you don't mind, of this seminal event," she went on, smugly. "We don't want to lose anything for posterity. After we finish, we will take a few more, though you will no longer be able to view them."

And she pulled out her cellphone and began taking Charles' picture from various angles, while Hans kept him under the shadow of his pistol.

"You have successfully evaded us for centuries, and now please excuse us if we gloat a bit in this triumph." By now, both her voice and her facial expression had changed from that of a curious reporter to a sinister, threatening, even guttural voice and countenance.

"When this ceremony ends, at least your part in it, we have a ritual that may go on for a while after you are gone. And I know that you will not begrudge our celebrating a bit, will you? So now, Hans, let's begin. Why don't you start with one leg, then another, then an arm, then another, and finally, we will get to some of the more essential parts. And at the end," she said, displaying a knife that she pulled from her bag, "we may have some more fun with you."

14

There was a pause of anticipation in the mountain hut as the two attackers smugly contemplated what was about to transpire. Charles, still bound, sat quietly, showing no emotion, but confident that Claudine was somewhere outside. Meanwhile, Marianne and Hans readied themselves for what they thought would forever be commemorated by *La Noche* as its greatest victory.

But the attackers could not have foreseen what happened next. The explosion from Claudine's high-powered rifle shattered the thin wooden door as one of its shells sank deeply into the lumbar region of Hans' back, showering splinters of the door and bits of Hans' bloody flesh inside the hut. With a look of surprise on his face, he took one step and then stumbled, the pistol firing harmlessly into the floor.

Marianne, taken off guard for only a moment, instinctively went to her back-up weapon of choice, the knife that she had already pulled from its bag, now with the intent of dispatching Charles by her own hand. She had originally planned to use this knife to produce a trophy of sorts, a piece of the Apostle John, something to put on display as a relic for the members of *La Noche de Oscuridad*. But now, with Claudine rushing into the hut, the knife was her only hope for self-defense.

As Claudine burst into the one-room hut, Marianne slashed at her with the knife, producing a serious gash in Claudine's left rib cage. Turning, Claudine grabbed at Marianne, pulling her down to the floor on top of Hans' body. Even with her wound, Claudine was a formidable opponent and Marianne, not being a person of great physical strength, sized her up quickly and decided to flee. She would have tried first to finish off Charles had she been able to find Hans' pistol, but fortunately for Charles, Hans had fallen on it.

As Marianne started for the door, Claudine caught her and wrestled her again to the floor, loudly grunting with an expression of pain and determination. All Marianne could do was to slash aimlessly with her now bloody knife. Striking again, this time on Claudine's right thigh, Marianne disabled her enough to prevent further attack and pursuit. As Claudine rolled over, moaning in the pain of her wounds, Marianne raced out the door, knife still in hand, down to her car and back down the mountain. Claudine, even in her crippled state, attempted to follow, but she was too hurt to go more than a few steps.

Charles could do no more than to watch the attack and hope for the best. Claudine, weakened and bleeding profusely from her wounds, struggled to untie him. And in the shock of the moment, all Charles could do was to feebly ask her, "Are you badly hurt?"

"Yes," came Claudine's standard monosyllabic reply. And losing consciousness, she crumbled to the floor. Charles briefly considered going after Marianne Weems but he knew that he must look after Claudine. Pursuing Marianne would have to wait.

■ ■ ■

Enrique, Millie and Frank arranged a teleconference with Dr. Chandler and Douglas Parks. Once everyone had been brought up to date, they began to explore options for their next steps.

"First," began Parks, "we must find out what is happening in France. We must do what we can to throw Weems and Oltorf off the trail. They have committed no crime, at least as far as we know, so we can't have them arrested and anyway, we must avoid involving the local police."

"If Charles Boutte has been killed, then our only remaining candidate is the man from England, I forgot his name," Dr. Chandler struggled to remember.

Parks replied, "His name is Geoffrey Smythe and he is a banker in Cambridge. Hans Oltorf and Hugh Matthews already visited him, coming away with the conclusion that he was not the Apostle John and must be a decoy."

"Yes," continued Dr. Chandler, "and we know that he is a decoy because his writings are so mixed, a combination of John-like pieces with others that are distinctly not John-like. So, I think that we can safely assume that he is not the Apostle John."

"I am not so sure that we can rule him out," contributed Enrique. "His mixed writings are no guarantee of anything at all. Since he seems to be the only remaining candidate, he will definitely be their target. And in the absence of further matches in our database, should he not be our target as well?"

"Then someone must go and visit him," replied Parks. "Millie, are you and Frank okay to make the trip?"

Millie and Frank exchanged glances and both began to wryly smile. "After what we've already been through," began Frank, "what more can happen? Yes, if it's acceptable to you, Millie, we will go." And Millie nodded in agreement.

"And," as an afterthought from Parks, "why don't you take Hugh Matthews with you? He's British, he's already visited Smythe once, and perhaps he can explain a bit about Oltorf that will help us find him."

"Where are you going now?" asked Randall in another of their abbreviated phone conversations.

"You know that I can't tell you," Millie replied, adding, "but I can tell you this; I think this project is coming to an end soon. When it does, I'll be able to tell you more."

"Then can you at least tell me in some vague and general way what you are actually doing?" He was getting increasingly agitated with being put off so easily.

"No," she replied, "but I will tell you that it's pretty boring work, no excitement, just one hum-drum day after another. Watching TV is more exciting than this. Ironing is more exciting than this. And this work is totally safe. You needn't worry that I will break a fingernail or something terrible like that." She had to admit to herself that she enjoyed spinning this story to Randall, and for some reason, she was getting better at sarcasm.

After landing at Heathrow, Millie and Frank boarded the train to Cambridge, where they would meet up with Hugh Matthews. The trip took them out of the city and into the lush green of the English country-side. Both of them found time to relax on their way, at least temporarily putting off any worry about one more encounter with a John candidate. Millie thought to herself that so far, she had a pretty poor batting average: Father Cardenas was dead, Charles Boutte missing and possibly dead, and neither of them was the man she was seeking. Perhaps the third time, with Geoffrey Smythe, would be different. She could only hope.

She was encouraged by her last visit with Juan before leaving for England. Meeting him early in the morning, she asked Juan to pray for her. He was eager to do so, and kneeling together in the little chapel, he began:

"Father God, we humbly ask you to look with favor upon this child of yours, Millie. She has experienced your great light and truth, and the life you freely give us. But she has also suffered great pain. I beseech you to turn her pain into joy: joy and wonder, and the freedom that comes with your truth, a truth that lives in the hearts of all who love you. This child of yours, Millie, has come to learn your voice, the voice of the Good Shepherd. I pray that you will lead her to good pasture and to the water that springs up and from which she will never thirst again. And keep her from the evil one, as she seeks to obey this calling that you have placed on her. I ask all of this in the name of the one who is always working, our Lord Jesus Christ. Amen."

Keeping this prayer close to her heart, Millie was ready for one last trip. At least she hoped it was her last trip.

Hugh Matthews, the fifth member of the original team, met Millie and Frank at the station in Cambridge. They had met him only once before, at the original team orientation. His greeting was warm and he seemed eager to brief them on Geoffrey Smythe. Millie and Frank would be careful with their questions about Hans Oltorf, hoping to get an objective response from Hugh without revealing what they had learned from Parks. For all they knew, of course, Matthews might be allied with Oltorf and Weems. No one, it seemed, was beyond suspicion at this point.

However, during their conversation Frank received a text message from Douglas Parks. Oltorf was dead, Weems was missing, and Charles was okay. Claudine was seriously wounded, but would recover. Parks wanted to know how Matthews reacted when he heard the news.

"Hans Oltorf? He seemed quite reserved, didn't say much, allowed me to take the lead. Seemed a tad 'mousey' if you ask me." That was all that Professor Hugh Matthews had to offer regarding Oltorf. His demeanor revealed no particular reaction when Frank reported that Oltorf had been killed during an attempt on the life of another John candidate.

"You don't say. Well that is quite troubling, isn't it? Sort of makes one wonder who can be trusted in this affair, doesn't it?"

Millie immediately liked Hugh Matthews, his British reserve hiding what she imagined was a very dry but very healthy sense of humor. Neither she nor Frank felt any suspicion that he might be one of the infiltrators.

"Geoffrey Smythe, yes, I can tell you about him: a solicitor for a local bank, trained in the area of trusts and estates. He is a lay reader in his local Anglican church, you know, and active in church affairs here in Britain. Since I'm on faculty here at the university, our paths have crossed at times over the years. Not much interest in Shakespeare, I'm afraid, but we can't all be enlightened by the Bard, now can we?"

"What about his writings?" inquired Millie.

"Yes, you see, they were quite mixed. I hadn't understood at first how unusual that was, until hearing it from Douglas Parks. His legal writings had no correspondence to the Apostle John's. Dreadful, boring things they are, all about complicated ways to avoid paying taxes, I imagine. Matters that bankers and solicitors discuss over brandies at their club. But his spiritual writings, which include a novel in the genre of C.S. Lewis, are quite absorbing. And they match perfectly to those of our beloved Apostle John.

"I found him to be a bit stuffy, and arrogant," Matthews went on, "but wouldn't those adjectives apply to virtually all solicitors? We certainly can't hold that against him, now can we? And given that, he would no doubt seem to be the last person on earth to be a first century apostle. After all, the writer of a gospel in the Bible posing as a solicitor? My word! God himself couldn't be that devious!"

"Do you believe, Hugh, that Smythe has a guardian or protector?" asked Frank. "You understand, do you not, that the other two candidates who we've interviewed did have such protection. In one case, that protection failed and the candidate was murdered. The other protector actually saved the candidate's life; in point of fact, by killing Hans Oltorf and fending off Marianne Weems."

"We must ask Geoff," responded Matthews. "I saw no evidence of such a person. But it would seem that such a protector might come in handy in light of what's happened with the other candidates. I believe Oltorf and I were a bit thrown off by the mixed nature of Geoff's writings. But now with the pool of candidates unfortunately dwindling, I fear that he can expect a visit from Ms. Weems or some associate of hers."

An appointment was made with Geoffrey Smythe for the following morning. And coincidentally, Smythe had invited his guests to meet him at his club.

A final update was texted by Douglas Parks to both Millie and Frank. He always tried to keep his messages as cryptic as possible. It read: "Survivor of attack still at large with no known location. Body of dead attacker still unclaimed. Is your associate clean?"

Millie, struggling as always with a keyboard of any size, texted back simply "clean. Will know more tomorrow."

15

Millie and Frank were becoming old pros at the vagaries of interviewing John candidates. But they had learned early on that it was impossible to unequivocally confirm or deny the true identity of the candidate. Even a polygraph test would be inconclusive. Millie thought that it would have been so much easier had there been some higher authority with a 'little black book' itemizing all of the decoys, including their protectors, as well as the true Apostle John. But she understood that if such an authority existed, it would be deeply hidden, and would be extremely averse to sharing such secret information. Besides, Douglas Parks and Dr. Chandler had never even hinted at the existence of such an entity.

It had also occurred to Millie to check for the evidence of birth records for each candidate. Perhaps the true Apostle John would have no such records, having been born only once, in the first century. But then, who knew if he had lived straight through the centuries or if he had repeatedly died and been reborn as a different person?

As a result, Millie and Frank, along with Hugh, were left to make a subjective assessment, knowing that each candidate would be skilled at deception. Father Cardenas had certainly been convincing. She had been sure that he was John. But his death did not summon the Risen Christ, at least not yet. Killing each candidate to see what would happen next seemed to be a poor method of determining identity.

They had both sensed something about Charles Boutte that told them that he was not the Apostle John. Neither Millie nor Frank could say exactly why they were so sure. Of course, he could still be John, having now survived two assassination attempts. The *La Noche* people certainly must have thought that he was John, even if Millie and Frank did not. But neither Millie nor Frank believed that Charles was their man. Besides, neither one wanted to take on Claudine.

At this point, Geoffrey Smythe, perhaps the unlikeliest of the candidates, was left. They couldn't, however, allow their knowledge that he was the only remaining candidate to influence their thinking. Anyway, perhaps more matches would be found in the database, revealing more candidates to be checked out.

As arranged, they met Smythe at his club. It was certainly quite "clubby" with Scottish plaid carpeting on the floor, dark wood paneling on the walls and deep leather arm chairs. All that was missing was brandy and cigars. While smoking was banned (though still practiced in some private rooms), brandy was abundantly available; however, this was a morning meeting. Coffee, tea and cakes were served, but as the meeting progressed, they remained untouched.

From the beginning, the conversation with Smythe was strained.

Geoffrey started in a negative vein: "I thought that the first interview was sufficient to satisfy you, Professor Matthews, and yet, here we are again, with two new faces. Please explain your purpose in arranging this meeting." And he folded his arms and stopped speaking, leaving the three visitors to consider how to begin.

Frank broke the ice: "Yes, we know that you previously met with Professor Matthews and Hans Oltorf. But Millie and I are also on the interview team and we wanted to meet you as well."

"That answer simply does not satisfy me. You will have to do better than that," he replied and folded his arms again.

In the silence of the almost-empty club, it occurred to Millie that this meeting, so unlike her introductions in San Jose and France, was off to a very rocky start.

Geoffrey continued, this time directly to Millie and Frank, "I don't know why you are here but I must tell you that I have already shared all that I intend to share with Professor Matthews and Mr. Oltorf."

"Mr. Oltorf," responded Hugh, "is dead." And he paused to observe Smythe's reaction.

Smythe's face was emotionless, revealing nothing.

After another awkward pause, he rose as if to leave. "I believe this meeting is at an end. I am sorry that you have come all this way, but until you can explain to me why you are here and what you want from me, I have nothing more to say.

"If you like, I will make myself available to meet with you again to-morrow morning. Perhaps by then, you will be better prepared." And he walked out, leaving them alone in the club.

That evening, Millie, Frank and Hugh debriefed on their observations of Smythe from the brief meeting. It was painfully clear that Smythe would not be satisfied until they explained more.

Millie: "I felt cross-examined by him. While we didn't have a chance to ask any of our questions, his overall performance told me what I need to know. He is not the Apostle John. He just can't be. However, I do feel the need to advise him to be careful and if he lacks a protector, he needs to find one."

"Of course," countered Hugh, "perhaps his attitude and his demeanor are meant to protect him. Without a guardian as the others have had, per-haps this is the next best approach."

"We'll never be completely certain," added Frank. "But perhaps the best way to get a reaction from him is to treat him as if he is a decoy. I have to believe that he'll truly want to know more about Oltorf's death and what it might mean for him."

They returned to the club the following morning, hoping that Smythe would be more receptive to them.

Frank began: "Geoffrey, yes, we knew that you were previously interviewed by Professor Matthews and Hans Oltorf. And from that meeting it has been concluded that you are a decoy for the Apostle John. However, as we mentioned yesterday, much has happened since that interview. The death of Hans Oltorf is only the beginning.

"We must tell you, Geoffrey, that in addition to the death of Oltorf, one of your brother decoys has been murdered and another has survived no less than two assassination attempts."

At this, Smythe began to open up. "I was not aware of that. This news is very troubling to me. Do we know who is behind all of this?"

Another pause, before he went on, speaking in a louder, more plaintive voice, "I would like to know if I am in danger. Please explain yourself."

"Mr. Oltorf," continued Frank, "was an infiltrator, an enemy who was attempting to find the Apostle John and assassinate him. You are known as a John candidate to this infiltrator group, one member of which is still at large."

There was another uncomfortable silence. "I have understood," began Smythe, slowly, "that I am to reveal as little as possible to anyone, and that includes you. You must excuse my behavior yesterday.

"I have further understood," he continued in his dignified manner, "that I am to distract any enemy of John to me, in order to keep John hidden until the time that has been ordained for his death and the return of Christ, the Messiah.

"Now," he continued, "you are telling me that a very formidable enemy has come, an entire organization bent on the death of John. And that their search for John has led them into your inner circle, and deaths of decoys such as myself have resulted. Well, that is a revelation to me. I never dreamt that it would come to this. You see, I sincerely felt called to this role and I am prepared for whatever comes, except for my own death. Frankly, I never contemplated this.

"I need protection," he went on. "I always understood that there could be people who might like to harm the Apostle John, but really, it just seemed so remote to me at the time. Now, it's much more real. Perhaps it's only the cautious banker in me, but I want to manage my risk. Can you help me?"

All of this sounded sincere to Millie, though it did occur to her that his expressed fear would be an awfully good cover for the real Apostle John.

"Yes," responded Frank. "We'll report your request back to our leadership and see what we can do. For now, just continue to be cautious. And if you hear from someone named Marianne Weems, run like hell!"

"What a comfort you are," replied Smythe, with all the sarcasm he could muster. "I hope you can move swiftly. This whole affair has me a bit muddled. And even though you never really answered my questions about your role, I will try to be patient …. and careful."

Millie and Frank began the trip back to Spain, leaving Hugh to support Geoffrey Smyth as best he could. "I hope whoever chose Geoff for this decoy role knew what he was doing," Frank remarked, "and I hope that comment doesn't sound sacrilegious to you. Or maybe his attitude is part of the whole scheme. Oh, I don't know."

Millie could sympathize with both Geoffrey and Hugh. She had seen what the enemy could do firsthand and it was all right, in her opinion, to be afraid. And it was equally all right to complain. It's just that Geoffrey did so in such an unappealing way.

Back in Spain, Enrique was eager to hear from Millie and Frank. Once they assured him that Smythe was the least likely candidate to be the Apostle John, he eased into one of the comfortable chairs in his study and sipped on a glass of his private label Tempranillo.

"So, where do we go from here?" Frank asked, expressing the very same question that Millie was about to ask. "Are there any more candidates?"

"None that look promising," answered Enrique. "Douglas Parks has informed me that the analysts have found a number of new matches to the writings of the Apostle John, but they are quite random. None has a level of statistical probability that would justify further exploration. We are at a point where we must re-examine our assumptions and our methodology. And it would be a good thing to do so before any more lives are lost or imperiled."

Millie asked, "Has anyone heard further from Marianne Weems?" Millie shuddered a bit as she said the name.

"No," Enrique answered. "She seems to have vanished. Perhaps *La Noche* is also considering the very same thing as us: what have we learned and what can we do next? Olforf no doubt reported back to them about Smythe.

"*La Noche* has been in existence, in the shadows, for some time, searching as we have. They are good at it. We should not expect them to make a splash, or to do anything to make the headlines until they are very sure that they have their man. They have stumbled at least twice and that hurts their pride. Now is a time for introspection."

This whole conversation was deflating for Millie. After living for the past several months as if on a tightrope, the idea of re-examining assumptions and methodology seemed directionless. She wondered if the entire endeavor had hit a dead end. Thoughts of home began to crowd her mind.

Can I just go home now? Can I just pick up my life back home where I left off? I don't think so. So much has changed; so much so, that my life can never be what it was. I can't go back to that life.

Her thread had truly been pulled, and she was discovering that she was not the same person as before. Or maybe the real Millie had emerged from years of a false self, one that had worked for a time. In her heart, Millie knew that there was no going back, and that she could never simply pick up her old life where she had left it.

It wasn't only the experiences, the life on the edge, the adventure that she'd never known before. That was part of it. But at a deeper level, there was an awareness of a spiritual life that she'd never known to exist before.

It was a life of connection, of relationships. In a way beyond words, this experience had brought a vitality to her life that she found to be both exhilarating and authentic. And it was faith: faith in God who called her to this vaguely-defined mission, and also faith in the individuals God had placed in her path. And faith in herself – faith that if God had truly called her to this, then she must have had something to offer.

In a way, it was as if there had been a dance going on all along, all her life, one that she had just now discovered. And having discovered it, she could never go back, could never stop dancing and sit on the sidelines of life again. In a way, she felt like she was in the flow of a fast-moving stream and she didn't want to leave it.

However, after a brief check-in with Douglas Parks and Dr. Chandler, she was even more convinced that going home was the only thing left to do, though she would be leaving what felt like unfinished business. It seemed to her that God was not through with his work to re-shape her life, that although the thread had been pulled and pulled, there was a bit more pulling to do. Going home seemed like a return to another life, the life that she'd left behind. But what other options did she truly have?

And then she spotted Juan, puttering around outside the *hacienda*, working in the garden.

"Millie," he called out. "I have a proposition for you!"

16

"Juan, how are you feeling?" She was truly happy to see him, feeling a connection to him that went all the way back to Antigua.

"I am fine," he replied. "It will take much more than a bump on the head to slow me down for long. But I still grieve for Father Cardenas."

"Yes, it was such a loss. I know that you will feel the loss for a long time. Then are you planning to return to Antigua?" Now that Father Cardenas was gone, she wondered what might become of Juan. He had no one to protect. And she snickered under her breath as she thought of how he might fare as protector to Geoffrey Smythe.

"I don't know, my child. All I know is that I must pray and wait. The praying part is easy, of course, but the waiting part is very hard. I have faith that our Lord has something for me. But I cannot see it. My only hope is that he will reveal it soon. Our Lord, as you know by now, is full of surprises. And what about you, Millie? Will you continue your search?"

"I suppose I'm just as much in the dark as you, Juan. Our search for John seems to have failed and there appears to be no further opportunity for me. I suppose that I'll just go home and as you said, pray and wait."

Juan's face brightened. "Before you leave, Millie, I have a proposition for you. Would you consider joining me for a little walk? A walk on the *Camino de Santiago?*

"I made this pilgrimage years ago and now I would like to repeat it. Not the entire walk, mind you, for that might take months. But perhaps only the last stretch. We could take up the *Camino* about fifty kilometers out from Santiago de Compostela and over several days, perhaps a week, complete the pilgrimage. I can think of no better traveling companion than you, Millie. What do you say? You can always go home afterwards. But many people say that the pilgrimage is a deep spiritual experience, if you are willing to place yourself in the hands of God."

"I don't know, Juan. Remember, I'm not too good on rocky ground. I could wear my braces, but I might slow you down. I don't wish to start something and not be able to finish."

"Why don't you just hand your fears over to our Lord? He can get you through to your destination. Actually, we all need to trust that he can get us through to all of our destinations, whatever they may be. And besides, the pilgrimage is not about speed. Haven't you learned by now that your spiritual walk is more about taking your time and listening for that 'still small voice?'"

Even now, after so many experiences that required faith, Millie was unsure. She didn't want to disappoint Juan and if she was totally honest, she didn't want to disappoint herself or perform below her personal standards. So, she hesitated, even though the pilgrimage appealed to her deepening spirituality.

"You can do this, Millie." Juan was becoming her best cheerleader. "It would give joy to an old man."

"You may be old, Juan, but I'm not a hundred percent, as you know. I don't wish to be a burden to you." Her normally self-conscious nature was kicking in.

"I suppose that neither of us is at a hundred percent," he replied. "That's what makes us such a good pair. Between the two of us, we have one good pair of legs. If I hadn't wanted you to join me I would not have asked."

"Well, I have trusted the voices of others, others who I have respected, so far, and I have to say that I've never regretted a single moment, even the moments when I thought I had failed. So, when do we start?"

Juan was ready and answered quickly. "Tomorrow morning. I have already planned the trip, assuming that you would say yes. Enrique will have a driver take us to a good starting point. He'll also provide all the gear we'll need. Of course, it's important on this pilgrimage to travel light, and to be ready for whatever our Lord brings. It's much like Jesus told his disciples, to carry no second tunic, no money, and to allow the Lord to provide what is needed."

They left the following morning at dawn, but only after a hearty breakfast. Millie wondered if it might be their last good meal for days. Enrique's driver, Miguel, drove them to a way station on the *Camino* and let them out. Millie felt like she was in the middle of nowhere. But there was no going back. She would not disappoint Juan.

Their starting point was a *refugio*, or hostel, that served pilgrims on their way to Santiago de Compostela. At the hostel, they purchased a *credencial*, or passport ticket, that would be stamped at each way station along the Way of St. James, or *Camino*.

Millie immediately noticed a proliferation of scallop symbols, which she would continue to see throughout their pilgrimage.

"What is the significance of the scallop?" she asked Juan.

"The scallop," he replied, "is the symbol of St. James. There are various stories of the scallop and its association with him. One of those stories has the body of the saint, covered in these shells, washing up on the shore near Compostela. Some believe the grooves in the scallop represent the various paths that pilgrims take, converging on Santiago de Compostela. Shall we begin?"

"Can we begin with a prayer?" Millie sincerely wanted this to be a spiritual retreat for her as she contemplated her return home.

"Yes, of course," he replied. They knelt by the side of the path. "Holy Father," he began, "we need you. Your presence is both light and truth to us. As your children, we beseech you to guide us, protect us and watch over us as we seek to honor you with this journey of contemplation and adoration. Amen."

And they began, Juan using a staff as he walked, and Millie with her braces. They made an odd couple, she thought to herself, the old man and the middle-aged woman, both impaired, he by age and she by infirmity. Their backpacks contained the barest minimum in the way of a change of clothes and only one meal, a lunch that Enrique had provided for the first day.

At the first yellow *Camino* sign, the path veered off from the road and onto a rough trail. As they started, Millie contemplated the quiet, which was so refreshing to one who was accustomed to the ever-present hum of freeway noise. They were essentially alone, walking through a beautiful countryside, true pilgrims on a path to a far-off destination that they couldn't see.

Millie considered that this path, the *Camino de Santiago*, or Way of St. James, was not unlike her life path: she was walking – in a broader sense, living -- in a defined direction toward a destination in life that she couldn't see or in any real way, imagine. Way stations, provided by others, were placed along the way to help her stay on the path.

But in between, she and her companion must walk by faith, not by sight. They would need to stop for rest along their journey, and places for that rest would be provided by an unseen hand. They could walk at any pace, and they could stop and enjoy the vistas at any time. Eventually, they would reach the end of the path, but the true value would be in the journey itself.

They walked in quiet for over an hour before the silence was broken. By now the sun was high, radiating a warmth that seemed to penetrate deep inside of Millie.

"So, Juan, who was St. James?" she asked.

"He was one of the Twelve, an apostle of Jesus," replied Juan, "and the brother of the Apostle John, whom you are searching for. You can read about him in the gospels. He was a fisherman by trade, who was invited to follow Jesus."

"How is it that he is so important here in Spain? Didn't he live in the Holy Land?"

"There are a number of legends about him," Juan replied. "One legend has it that he came here to preach to the natives of this country, long before it was the Spain that we know today. He then returned home, instructed by a vision of the Virgin Mary. There, he was martyred by King Herod. This legend has his followers bringing his body back to Spain. Their ship foundered, and his body washed overboard, only to be later discovered intact on the beach, covered all over with the scallops that we see today."

"That doesn't sound too likely to me," answered Millie.

"The other story seems even less likely," Juan went on. "This legend has it that an angel piloted a ship bearing the body of James back here for burial. The ship's arrival interrupted a wedding taking place on the beach, prompting a horse carrying the bridegroom to rear, throwing both of them into the sea, only to rise again, covered with the scallops."

"Juan, do you believe in miracles?"

"Yes, my child, I do. I have a slightly more practical perspective on miracles, though. Our Lord works through miracles, no doubt. But if you will notice, he often uses the resources of men to complete them. For example, he didn't just feed the five thousand by producing food from thin air. No, he used the loaves and fishes that were offered to him. From this humble offering, he produced a miracle. I believe he is telling us that what we contribute is important, even if we think we have little to offer.

"Tell me, child, how are you doing on this trail?"

"Just clicking along," she replied, and for once Millie seemed to have lost her self-consciousness about her braces and her physical limitations.

As they walked, it seemed that weights were being lifted from her body; not so much in a physical sense, though she did feel stronger than she'd expected, traveling over the uneven terrain. But in a deeper sense, she felt uplifted. And very comforted to be traveling with Juan. The weight of her cares receded in a way that left her feeling as if a space was being carved out inside of her. That space was not left vacant, but was instead filled with a sweetness that she couldn't describe in words, but which was real nonetheless. Inexplicably, a smile came to her lips from a source deep within her. It remained for over an hour as they walked in silence.

They stopped for the lunch that Enrique had provided: pâté, cheese and hard-crusted bread, with some of his special Tempranillo. From time to time, other pilgrims passed them, with blessings exchanged as they went by. Millie was no longer concerned with their pace as she watched these younger pilgrims fade into the distance ahead of them.

As the day drew to a close, they came to another *refugio* or hostel, where they would spend the night. This was a simple affair, clean, but with no amenities. Soup was heating on a wood-fired stove, and it smelled delicious as Millie and Juan entered. Their *credencial* was stamped by an attendant, to whom they paid eight euros for the night.

The evening sky was clear and so before retiring, Millie and Juan went back outside.

"The Milky Way is another symbol of the *Camino*," Juan explained. "The legend tells us that the Milky Way was made from the dust raised up from the earliest pilgrims, beginning in the tenth century. Before the appearance of the scallop signs along the path, the Milky Way could be seen to point to Santiago de Compostela, helping pilgrims to navigate their way. And by the way, '*Compostela*' means 'field of stars.'"

Millie removed the braces from her legs. She was tired, and her hands were shaking a bit. But she no longer worried if she could complete this pilgrimage. And as she reflected on their first day's journey, she couldn't help but say a quick prayer of gratitude: *Thank you God, for this opportunity, the beauty, the solitude, and most of all, for Juan.*

17

The second day on the *Camino* saw them get off to an early start, not long after sunrise. Breakfast was spartan, including strong Spanish coffee, bread and honey. Traveling for the most part alone, their path led them through farms, near pens of sheep and horses.

Millie and Juan walked in silence for several hours, over rolling hills and fields with wooded borders.

"How did Santiago de Compostela become such a popular pilgrimage?" Millie wanted to know more history.

"It's quite an interesting story," Juan replied, "mostly based on a ninth century entrepreneur.

"You see," he went on, "the story goes that in the ninth century, a hermit monk discovered the remains of the Apostle James. He found them buried in a field, after witnessing strange lights in the sky above the field. How he knew that these remains were, in fact, the Apostle James, is lost to history. In any case, this was a time of economic difficulty. So, this enterprising monk decided that a shrine would be just the thing for the struggling village.

"Once the shrine received the blessings of the church fathers, it grew in popularity. Pilgrims began to come from all over Europe. Economic prosperity followed, with inns and other businesses springing up to serve the pilgrims. The cathedral that now stands in Santiago came after several earlier, smaller churches. By the eleventh century, business was booming and so a larger cathedral was needed."

"Maybe all of this," remarked Millie, "is another example of a miracle that needed a little help from a human, in this case, the hermit monk."

"Perhaps, my child, perhaps."

Small shrines, placed along the path, proved to be good places to stop and pray. Juan was always happy to pause. Millie found these stops helpful to re-center herself to the pilgrimage, and to her journey of faith. In between, her mind continued to drift away to thoughts of Randall, her children, and to her dismay, Marianne Weems, who seemed to be a dominant presence in the back of Millie's mind. Just as she began to worry about her perceived failure in the search for John, Marianne's face crowded into her thoughts. The shrines served to help Millie to clear her mind of these unwelcome images and re-center herself.

It took the full second day of walking in solitude to flush the noise from Millie's mind. Finally, as they approached the next hostel, where they would spend the night, she felt a peace that seemed to flood both her body and her mind. The random thoughts that had been plaguing her began to dissipate, finding their way into a sort of subconscious dumping ground.

Millie's attention and her presence were now much more focused. It was as if she was experiencing a light that was not physical, but which shone in a dimension beyond visual perception. The light was inner, unavailable to the eyes, but shining nonetheless. And it seemed to connect outward from Millie to Juan and in an odd sort of way, to all of creation.

Millie also noted the pungent smell of plowed soil, and of farm animals, flowers and crops that reminded her of Plostina. Surprisingly, this smell opened all of her senses to consider the blessings of creation, connecting her to life in a way she'd not felt since childhood. The disjointed compartments of her adult life were melting away, replaced by a feeling of wholeness, as if everything belonged to the life that God had created for her. It felt as if she could literally inhale this deeper sense of life as they walked.

As Millie and Juan reflected on their day, she tried to describe to him what she was experiencing. But she struggled to put it into words.

"Millie, it is impossible to describe spiritual experiences using human vocabulary. As our friend the Apostle Paul tells us, the Spirit speaks in sighs too deep for words. I know that the Spirit is speaking to you, and that you are experiencing something wonderful. It is all right to just leave it at that. Our human tendency is to want to analyze and describe every-thing, but in the spiritual world that is not necessary. The experience itself is enough.

"Love," he went on, "is the language of our faith. And it needs no words."

The next day, their third, was the quietest. Millie's questions were receding into the background, waiting for another day. One question re-mained, a question that she could not yet bring herself to ask.

The terrain was becoming hillier as they began to approach Santiago. More pilgrims appeared on their path, all traveling at a pace faster than that of Millie and Juan. Millie was happy to see them pass by. By now, she had seven scallop stamps on her *credencial*. Juan, she could see, was tiring, but she, even in her braces, was surprisingly, gaining strength. She wished for this pilgrimage to go on forever, so she slowed to Juan's pace. By now, she fully understood that the pilgrimage was not about speed.

The somewhat primitive conditions of the hostels were not a prob-lem. Everything spoke of simplicity and she began to truly appreciate the lack of amenities, such as hot water, that she had once found so essential.

The days were blurring together as well, with little sense of time, other than the celestial signs of the sun, moon and of course, the Milky Way, still pointing west to Santiago. Millie wondered if perhaps this was how the magi felt, following the star on their way to Bethlehem.

On the morning of the fourth day, they set out as before, after a break-fast that included potatoes, hard-crusted bread, jam and coffee. Fewer words were spoken, and yet Millie felt even closer to Juan as they silently walked the trail. In the late morning, she was able to spot the twin spires of the cathedral, still a long distance away. Millie had in her own way hoped that they might have one more day with no destination in sight. To her, the *Camino* seemed to call them to trust only in their faith as a guide.

She did not share her observation with Juan, who seemed to walk with his gaze downward most of the time, deep in contemplation.

The prayer stops at the shrines, no longer necessary for Millie to re-center, still provided some time for Juan to rest, as he was clearly tiring. Millie's prayers focused more and more on him, and on her final question of him, which had been gestating in her for the past day. Millie was not sure that she could ask it and yet, she was not sure that she could not. She did not wish her question to unsettle an old man whom she clearly had grown to love.

"Millie," he broke the silence as they walked, "I have been thinking of Father Cardenas. He was my good friend. I still grieve his loss. And I failed him." He sighed and paused before continuing. "I failed him, Millie. I should have protected him.

"Our Lord has told us that on that day, the day that he returns, those in the graves will hear his voice. Think of it! They will hear his voice! Those of us still living will hear a great trumpet sound. We will see our Lord riding on the clouds, with the angels all around him. Every eye will see him. Every ear will hear his voice. Can you imagine it, Millie?

"Even though I still grieve, I long for that day when Father Cardenas will hear the voice of our Lord. It gives me great comfort to know that it is coming. And it's coming for you and me, too, Millie. Only we don't know when. We won't know until he comes.

"In the meantime, we must go on, mustn't we? We must continue to live each day, to obey, and to love. And we must continue to allow ourselves to be fed where and when our Lord chooses to feed us. This pilgrimage, this journey of faith that we are sharing, has it fed you?"

"Yes," Millie replied, not needing to elaborate. "I am so grateful that you invited me to join you, and now I understand why it was better that I did not know what to expect. You are a wise man, Juan."

"A wise man? No. Well, I have lived a long time. I should be wise. But when I was younger, you see, I was not so wise. No. In truth, I was quite impulsive. Several times, my brashness offended one whom I deeply loved. My brother and I did that. My brother, the one who is now gone.

"We said and did things that we wish we could have taken back. The one whom we offended even gave us nicknames that meant that we were too full of ourselves, too zealous for our own good. And the worst of it came when he was troubled about his own fate. Yes, he was so troubled. But all we could think of was ourselves, our own glory, not our friend and his troubles. That was wrong, Millie, so wrong.

"But you know, Millie, even though we committed great offenses, our friend still loved us. He did. He truly did. And he forgave us for our arrogance. Believe it or not, we continued to be called to important work for our friend. We were not excluded and we did not have to earn our way back into our friend's good graces. No, we didn't. That's pretty remarkable, isn't it, Millie?"

"Yes it is," she replied, suddenly thinking of Randall.

They found another hostel and stopped for the night. Other pilgrims joined them, expressing excitement about their proximity to Santiago de Compostela and the final leg of the pilgrimage. Yet Millie found herself wishing that she and Juan had many more days to go. But time was running out on this experience, and she intended to do her best to savor what was left of it.

As she lay awake, Millie remembered Juan's words, how he had been called to important work, despite his own shortcomings and failures. She considered her own path that had brought her to this point, how the challenges of her life had seemingly disqualified her from any serious calling. Her strained marriage, her physical limitations and what she saw as her failures in this project should have rendered her useless to any important work.

And yet, here she was, despite everything, persevering down a path with no clear end, no real definition of success, walking solely on faith. Her calling, as undefined as it was, had remained as strong and compelling as ever.

The next morning, their fifth on the Camino, brought fog and the threat of rain. A cold breeze blew from the west, and clouds shrouded any view of the cathedral. Millie was thankful for that, enjoying the mystery of walking in a fog, as if she were encased in a cloud of faith.

They spoke little during the morning. By now, each of them could sense the mood of the other with no spoken words. Millie could tell that Juan was deep in prayer as he walked. And she, too, found herself in a sort of dream state, in a way, listening into the special silence that comes with fog.

By noon, the fog was burning off and a hazy sun could be seen through the clouds. Still, there was no sign of the cathedral. In her previous life, Millie would have fretted over their progress, or lack thereof. And she would have been anxious about losing the trail and possibly getting lost. But now, she was able to take what came and see God in the entirety of the created world around her. It was all coming together in a sort of unity that she could not explain.

"Millie." Juan had something to say and at this point in their journey, all small talk was far behind them.

"There is something that I need to tell you, Millie. Yes, it's time."

"You don't need to tell me, Juan, I know."

He went on, as if he hadn't heard her response. "I was not the person who you thought I was in Antiqua. I am not the person who I appear to be, even today. I was not the protector for Victor Cardenas. No. Not at all. Actually, he was the protector for me. That's what he was called to be, my protector. He did not write those sermons, the ones that were published. I did."

"Yes, Juan." She knew that no response was needed to his confession. "There is no greater love for a person than to lay down one's life for a friend. And Father Cardenas was your friend. But Juan, you would have done the same for him, wouldn't you? You tried, didn't you? Yes, you tried to save him."

"Yes, he laid down his life for me. For me." And Juan began to softly weep. "He was not the first one to do that. My friend, the one I offended so long ago, he did that too. He died for me. He died for me, Millie. I watched him die. I watched both of them die. And I know that is what he meant to do. But I offended him. I sinned against him. And he not only died for me, he used me in his work as if I had done no wrong.

"It just makes me feel so unworthy. I am unworthy, Millie. Unworthy. I should have been the one to die. I would have gladly died. But he won't let me die. He won't let me die, Millie. He won't let me die."

Millie, now also weeping, responded, "Your worth, Juan, is not measured by what you have or haven't done. It's not about that, Juan. Your worth is measured by the price he paid for you, by the love he gave to you. You are the disciple whom he loved."

As Millie spoke these words she contemplated what was happening, and the unreal nature of it. Here she was, walking with the Apostle John, who was still living after two thousand years. His heart was heavy in guilt and amazingly, it was Millie, the girl from Plostina, Millie, the wife and mother, Millie, the damaged woman who wore braces on her legs, who was comforting this despondent saint.

And as she gave Juan a long and tender hug, her thoughts went back to Father Vlacek, back in Plostina:

> *"Millie, you're just a dangling thread. There's more to you than anyone knows. And some day, someone will pull that thread. And when that happens, we will all find out how special you really are."*

18

That night, after their supper, they went back outside for one last view of the Milky Way. A cloud cover, however, kept it hidden. Instead, their vision was drawn to the west, where the lights of Santiago de Compostela reflected off the cloud bottoms. Despite its beauty, it was an ominous sight to Millie. Tomorrow would be the final day of their mini-pilgrimage. She was not ready for it to end.

For Millie, the pain of separation was already beginning. As she lay in bed, unable to sleep, she began to sob.

Juan turned to her. "So, my child, we are coming to the end of our pilgrimage, when we must say good-bye. How should we part?"

"I don't wish to part, Juan. Must we?"

"Yes, my child. You must return to Enrique, and then on to your home in America. I must travel in a different direction. You cannot follow me. You would be in great danger if you did.

"Now pray with me." And she reached out her hand, shaking a bit, holding his. The tighter she held on, the more her hand shook. He did not comment, but allowed her hand to grip his in a love embrace.

"Holy Father, we are like lost sheep without you, wandering through this precious life that you have freely given us. We go through the motions of living, listening to voices other than the voice of the Good Shepherd, your voice. Then, just as things appear so dark, we hear your voice and we see your light. You have blessed me with this child of yours, Millie, in whose face I see your light; the light of love that came into the world to live with us. I see in her some of your fullness, the fullness in which we all share. Holy Father, this child of yours has many rivers yet to cross. Keep her close to you, I pray. Feed her with your very person, strengthen her with your very self. Connect her branch firmly to your vine and never let her go. Watch over her and when her time comes, bring her home to the many mansions that you have promised to those who love you. Amen."

The next morning broke clear and cold. Gathering her things for their final stretch into the city, Millie felt as if she were moving in slow motion. The cares that had been driven out during their walk were now crowding back into her conscious thoughts. There were no more shrines to help her re-center as they entered the outskirts of Santiago. The smells of earth and animals and flowers were replaced by smells of the city.

After days in the country, walking on city streets seemed surreal. Shops were open. There was street noise, and vehicles of all kinds. Most of the streets were cobblestone, making Millie's walk much more difficult. Now and then, they could see the cathedral, looming behind the buildings on the narrow streets, coming ever closer. Millie had no idea of its size until they were within a few blocks and she had an unobstructed view.

"It's so huge!" she exclaimed as they walked up a street that point-ed directly to the cathedral. The mostly Romanesque cathedral loomed above them, dark and in a way, majestic. But not warm and inviting. It looked impressive, but also somewhat forbidding to Millie.

"Yes," replied Juan. "In the medieval times, there was a sort of com-petition among the cities of Europe. Today, they take the most pride in their football team. In the middle ages, their cathedral was the focal point, and each city tried to outdo the others."

The cathedral was on one side of a large open square or plaza, its or-nate spires reaching up hundreds of feet. On the open plaza were other pilgrims, some literally lying down on the pavement, others on their knees in prayer. The great anti-climax of the destination was the austere interior of the church, including the remains of the Apostle James, the brother of

John. It was possible to view the box containing his remains below the altar. And so Millie went in, while Juan rested on the steps outside.

Millie returned to Juan outside the cathedral. "I have to say, Juan, that my time inside was a bit of a letdown. Actually, I'm not sure what I expected. But I'm not going to allow my brief time inside the cathedral to lessen the deep spiritual experience I shared with you on the pilgrimage."

"I am glad," Juan commented, "that the meaning of this pilgrimage for you was not in its destination, but in the journey itself."

"Yes, of course, and in my walking companion."

Enrique had booked them into one of the nicer *paradors* (state-owned hotels) in Santiago. The amenities of a first class hotel seemed strange to Millie after her pilgrimage experience. And the noise of the city was uncomfortable compared to the peaceful quiet of the pilgrimage trail. However, she had to confess that she did look forward to a hot bath and a good meal in the hotel restaurant. She could finally take off her braces.

Juan looked refreshed as they sat and enjoyed a wonderful meal of steak, fresh vegetables and a good Rioja. Their conversation retreated to small talk. Now that Juan's identity was out in the open, Millie's curiosity could have prompted literally thousands of questions that would be of interest to the entire planet. But her respect and affection for Juan outweighed her curiosity. She had become so close to him that it was enough to trust that he would tell her whatever he thought was important. And rather than expose the past, it seemed better to live in the present, knowing that her time with him was short.

The sounds and visual stimulation of the restaurant were a bit much for Millie and she knew that she would need to go through a sort of re-entry process. It was tempting to try to hold onto the feelings that she had experienced on the pilgrimage trail. But that would be impossible. The pilgrimage was a once-in-a-lifetime experience. Perhaps she could return to those feelings again sometime in the future. Now, however, she felt invaded, and a bit overwhelmed, by so many sights and sounds.

And just as she was wondering how long it would take to readjust to her twenty-first century world, she spotted a familiar face across the restaurant. Just for a moment, and almost in the blink of an eye, she saw a woman sitting alone at a table in the shadows. A woman who appeared to be Marianne Weems.

Waiters and guests were coming and going and by the time Millie's field of vision cleared again, the woman was gone. But they had made eye contact. The woman, who she was sure was Marianne, knew that she'd been spotted. So it was obvious that she did not wish to be seen, at least not by Millie.

Millie debated in her own mind if she should tell Juan. She decided not to tell him. For the time being, she would be Juan's protector. The thought pleased her.

Enrique had left a message for Millie. Miguel was to pick her up the next morning and return her to his *hacienda*. From there, she had no idea where she might go.

She phoned Randall. "I'm probably coming home soon," she began. "My work here is ending."

"I hope it was a success," he offered, "though I have no idea what 'success' actually means for your mysterious project. Anyway, I hope you found the two-thousand year-old man you were searching for. Oh, and by the way, I need to tell you that I got a few more calls from that lady, Marianne Weems. I think she finally believed me when I kept telling her that I didn't know where you were. All she would say was that there were others who might help her find you. Has she found you, Millie?"

"Yes," Millie answered in a distant way, "I believe she has."

"I want to start over with you, Millie. I want our marriage to work. Changes are needed, I know, mostly from me. I want to start again to meet the Millie who's gone off to this strange project. I'm not sure that I truly know that Millie and maybe I've mistaken you for someone else all along. Maybe in fact, I've been wrong about who you are. Does that make sense? Are you willing to try?"

"Yes, Randall. I understand, and I am also willing to try. But first I need to finish something here. Then I will come home and we'll start again. You are right; I'm not the person you thought I was. Actually, I too have discovered that I'm not the person who I thought I was."

Millie spent a restless night in bed, worrying about Marianne Weems and what might happen in the morning. She had moved to a room adjoining Juan's and before going to bed, she reminded him to be sure to lock his door and not open it for anyone who might knock. He had not asked her why she was concerned.

By 6:00 a.m. she was dressed, packed and ready to meet Juan for breakfast. She hoped that the early hour would help them to avoid Marianne. Miguel was to come for her at 9:00 so she knew that they would have time to kill after breakfast. But hopefully, they could find a safe place until Miguel arrived.

The hotel restaurant was nearly empty when Millie met Juan for breakfast. While Millie had succeeded in refraining from asking him too many questions, there was one that she could not hold back: "Juan, will I ever see you again?"

"I hope so, my child, but I doubt it. This existence has been a lonely one for me. My brothers all died long ago. They now live in the glory of the light of Christ, united in love with our Lord. But not me. Not me. Only I have been left behind -- alone -- the last eyewitness to the word made flesh.

"I was there. I was there, Millie. He called me, along with my brother, from our fishing boat. I saw him every day, heard him, touched him. He washed my feet. He fed me. These eyes, my eyes, Millie, saw him transfigured into dazzling light. And these eyes, my eyes, also watched him die. He died. I saw it. I was there. And yet he lives. I saw him alive again!

"I long to be reunited with him, Millie. And also with my brothers. This has been my wish for two thousand years.

"Over the centuries, I have met and loved many people. But it was difficult to get close to them. And then, of course, they died and I did not. I wanted to be a witness to our Lord, but in an inconspicuous way. So my writings have used names other than my own and I have tried not to draw attention to myself. I do not wish to be a novelty, or a celebrity of any kind. I do not wish to be interviewed on television or the newscasts. And so I have been careful to keep my identity private, while still serving as I have been called to serve.

"My life after today will be in another location, one that I cannot reveal. Helpers are available to me, to arrange everything, including more decoys and protectors. It would be dangerous for everyone if I told you their names. But I want you to know that you should not worry about me. I will be fine. I will be safe. But I will miss you, Millie, I will miss you. I will truly miss you. You are a gift from him, Millie, a gift to help me ease the pain of separation from him.

"Let me promise you this: I will find a way to contact you, once I have found my next location. Expect the unexpected. I may stand at your door and knock. Look for me.

"Our Lord has promised us that we will have pain, and I can tell you that saying good bye to you, Millie, is truly painful for me. But He also promised that our pain will turn into joy. So let us look forward with the expectation of joy."

Millie was choking back the tears. Parting from Juan was proving to be painful beyond measure.

"There is little more that I can say, Juan. You know that I love you. And it gives me great joy to hope that we might meet again. I will be waiting."

Millie found it hard to finish her breakfast. As she looked up at Juan, clearing the tears from her eyes, she spotted a familiar figure entering the restaurant and taking a seat by the windows. Marianne, sitting alone, was quickly served a cup of coffee, which sat untouched on her table. She was dressed in traveling clothes, as one would wear to leave for the airport on a business trip. Beside her on the table was a large travel bag. And as she and Millie made eye contact, she sipped her coffee, picked up her travel bag, rose from her table and began to walk toward Juan and Millie.

19

Marianne walked slowly and purposefully across the restaurant toward Millie's table, showing no emotion, but clearly focused on Millie and Juan. She might have been coming across the room to greet a slight acquaintance, one whom she barely knew. Clutching her travel bag in one hand, she held her other hand behind it, as if to hide something.

Millie quickly decided not to say anything to Juan, who would have had little chance to escape on his own power. She hoped that her face betrayed no alarm as Marianne approached. But there was no avoiding an awkward moment of silence with Juan, causing him to look up as if he were expecting her to say something.

If Marianne had been carrying a gun in her hidden hand, she could easily reveal it now and shoot with little risk of missing. So Millie decided, when Marianne was still about ten feet away, to spring into her defense of Juan.

Without a word, and with considerable stiffness in her unbraced legs, she jumped up from her seat as quickly as her legs would take her, and moved between Marianne and Juan, blocking Marianne's path of attack. As she took her position of defense, Juan began to turn and look to see what was happening.

And now the emotion of the attack exploded in the calm of the quiet restaurant.

"Get out of my way, Millie! You will not prevent this! Get out of my way or you will die too! You cannot stop me! Get out of my way!"

Without speaking, Millie braced herself.

Juan had now turned in his chair, and could see the drama unfolding. Reminiscent of his failed attempt to protect Victor Cardenas in San Jose, he rose and cried out: "Noooo, nooo! Do not do this! Do not do this! Millie! Get away! Get away!"

The situation had quickly escalated beyond Marianne's original plan, sending her into a state of panic. So she hurriedly and awkwardly lunged toward Juan, who was by now attempting to pull Millie out of the way of the attack. As she lunged, Marianne pulled a knife from behind her travel bag, the same knife she'd used to attack Charles Boutte and Claudine.

Marianne's lunge badly missed both Millie and Juan, and she began to lose her balance. Straightening up, she turned, and as she did, both Millie and Juan turned with her. Millie was determined to do whatever it took to use her body to shield Juan and block Marianne's path of attack. All the while, Juan, still behind Millie, tried to pull her out of the way and to safety. Only two feet now separated the three actors in a contorted dance of death.

Marianne lunged again toward Juan, the knife once more seeking its mark. Millie stepped forward, directly into its path, the knife plunging into her right shoulder, and then ripping downward in a deep slice through her upper arm.

Seriously wounded and struggling to keep standing, Millie reached toward Marianne to push her back, all the while keeping Juan behind her. They pushed at each other for a moment in a strange back and forth motion. But finally, losing consciousness, she began to crumple to the floor, whispering as she fell, "This will not pass! You will not succeed! This is in the Lord's hands."

Marianne, breathing heavily under the emotion of her battle with Millie, could now view her target unobstructed by his defender. While she would have liked to relish the moment, she knew that she must act quickly.

She would only allow herself to say, "At long last!" before she went at Juan, who, not attempting to escape or fight, was now bending down to tend to Millie, whose blood was flooding out of her shoulder and arm and onto the carpeted floor. And as Marianne moved to point blank range, she pulled back the now bloody knife, poised for a fatal strike. The scene was eerily reminiscent of the assassination in San Jose.

Just then two strong arms, coming from behind Marianne like a pincer, wrapped tightly around her, locking both arms to her sides. Miguel, Enrique's driver and sometime bodyguard, had stepped in from the entrance of the restaurant, quickly assessed the situation, and moved to render Marianne immobilized and helpless. The knife fell harmlessly to the floor.

Unaware of Miguel's rescue, Millie finally lost consciousness, her last words, "Juan! Juan!" And then darkness, a darkness unlike any she had ever known.

■ ■ ■

Millie opened her eyes. She was in a soft bed, in a plush bedroom, at a location vaguely familiar to her. Enrique's *hacienda* was not where she expected to find herself, but there she was. With no sense of the passage of time, she strained to remember the events that must have led her here. In her memory, there was a dim recollection of breakfast in a hotel restaurant, and the expectation of a sad parting from Juan.

And then, as if emerging from a fog, the details of the attack began to come together in her memory. And immediately, she faded out again.

Days passed before she re-awakened. This time, Enrique and Frank were at her bedside. "Millie," Frank began, "you've been coming in and out of consciousness. Please stay with us. We've been afraid we might lose you."

And so the explanations began, Enrique taking the lead.

"Where do I begin?" he asked rhetorically. "Ah, I know," he said, attempting to inject some humor into the somber atmosphere of the bedroom. "I will begin at the beginning."

Millie was too weak to smile and too afraid to ask what she desperately wanted to know. She wanted to know what happened to Juan but knew she'd have to wait until Enrique came to the point.

"Let me begin, first of all," Enrique started, "to let you know that Juan is all right. He survived the attack unscathed, which is more than we can say for you, Millie."

Finding it hard to speak, Millie simply breathed a sigh of relief.

"You may remember, Millie," Enrique continued, "that while you were on the pilgrimage, quite a few others passed you on the way. You probably thought that they were just average people, seeking a closer relationship with our Lord by walking the *Camino*. Well, of course, most of them were. But some of them were my people, watching you and Juan, making sure that you were safe. They were prepared to defend you against any attack while you walked the pilgrimage. You didn't know that, did you, Millie?"

He answered his own question, "Of course you didn't. How could you? And when you reached Santiago, Miguel was already there, making sure that any threats against you would be taken care of. He watched your every step, Millie.

"Miguel was the one who came into the restaurant and dealt with Marianne Weems, just after she attacked you. It's a pity he couldn't have been thirty seconds quicker or else you'd not be here in my *hacienda*, trying to recover from your severe wounds."

"You have been seriously injured, Millie," Frank interjected. "Miguel did not want to take you to a local hospital out of fear that other attackers might be lurking around. So, he quickly got you bandaged up and drove you here, to Enrique's *hacienda*. You've been patched up, but the damage to your shoulder and arm will require reconstructive surgery and rehabilitation that are quite impossible out here in the country. We'll have to get you back to the States for that, as soon as you can travel."

"It has been a week since the attack," Enrique continued. "Once you are strong enough, we'll get you up and prepare you for returning home.

"Oh and one more thing, Millie. Marianne Weems is in custody. I do not believe you will need to worry about her again. I have arranged it so that you will not need to testify. Nor will Juan."

"You did a very brave thing, Millie," added Frank. "Bless you for doing what you did. I don't know many people who would act with the courage that you showed."

"Yes," Enrique went on. "There is a lot more to you, Millie, than appears on the surface."

"I know, I know, so it would seem," came her soft response. "Someone long ago told me that. I don't believe I knew what it meant at the time."

Enrique and Frank left to give Millie time to rest. She was still too semi-conscious to ask the deeper questions that would eventually need to be answered.

Later in the afternoon, Enrique returned, alone. Millie was now sitting up in bed and taking some soup. Her right arm was virtually useless, the muscles torn by Marianne's attack. She was awkwardly using her left hand to eat the soup. Overall, though, Millie was feeling stronger and more alert.

"Millie," began Enrique, "I know that you must want to know about Juan, what has happened to him, where he has gone, and so forth. I must tell you that he is all right, though very concerned about you. He so much wanted to come here to help us nurse you back to health. But that might have been dangerous. He would have been safe here, of course, as we have many strong defenses that you may not have previously noticed. But eventually, he would have to leave and we just could not have our enemies waiting outside our gates, now could we?

"Juan has been taken to a new locale, one where he will be safe. I cannot tell even you where it is, mostly to protect you from any, shall we say, unpleasant encounters in the future."

"Before leaving, Juan wrote you a letter and left it with me. I will bring it to you later. But before I do, and before Frank returns, we need to have a little more conversation.

"You will be returning soon to America for further medical attention and of course, to resume your life at home. Once you return, you will no doubt be met by Douglas Parks and Dr. Chandler, who will expect you to share every detail of your experience here in Spain.

"Of course, they will want to know about Charles Boutte, and you will tell them that he is not John the Apostle. Likewise they will want to know about Geoffrey Smythe, assuming that Hugh Matthews has not already told them that Geoffrey is also not John.

"You must choose, Millie, if you will or will not tell them about Juan, that it is Juan who is the Apostle John. If you tell them, they will be surprised. They do not expect it. They will likely not even ask you about Juan. But if you choose to tell them, they will be very happy. It will prove their theory. They will write papers on it and the publicity will be significant. And you, Millie, will become famous. 'The woman who discovered the Apostle John, after two thousand years of hiding.'

"You understand, of course, how difficult this would make it for us to continue to protect Juan, to keep him hidden until the proper time. It is up to you, Millie. You must decide. I have not told Frank. He still believes that Juan is just an old friend, the sexton at the church in San Jose, and the protector of my cousin Victor. Frank believes that Marianne's attack was aimed not at Juan but at you, Millie, to get you out of the way of any future interference with *La Noche*.

"It comes down to this, Millie: you may choose to reveal our secrets or to keep them. Juan's safety is in your hands. It is up to you Millie, so please think about it. Do you have any questions?"

"Yes, Enrique, I do have one question" Millie spoke slowly and softly. "You told me before that you were part of the foundation that sponsored our research. If you are interested in protecting Juan instead of exposing him, why did you help sponsor our project?"

"It is always easier, and more effective, Millie," replied Enrique, "to operate on the inside of a project such as this, than to try to influence it from the outside. Yes, I have helped to sponsor the project. And Douglas Parks and Dr. Chandler are very interested in the scientific application behind it. Let us say that I am also interested in the science of the project, though only mildly, I must confess. My greater interest, you see, is in the spiritual application of the project. Thanks to you, Millie, the spiritual application has been protected, all the while you have contributed to the science."

"I understand," she replied. "Then you can be assured, Enrique, that I will continue to protect the spiritual application of this project. Please do not worry about that. I have no desire to be famous and I will not betray a friend. Juan's secrets are safe with me."

"I will now bring you Juan's letter, Millie."

20

Millie was asleep when Enrique returned. He left Juan's letter on the table by her bed. Hours later, when she awoke, she found it, a small envelope with her name written on its cover.

Inside, she found Juan's letter. She awkwardly opened it with her good hand.

Juan's letter read as follows:

> *Millie, I hope and pray that you are recovering from your wounds. I could only wish that you had been spared, just as I had wished for Father Cardenas. You are a person of great worth to me, and I would have gladly put myself in your place and taken the knife blow.*
>
> *My lifetime has been a long thread, one which has stretched from that day on the beach, when Jesus told my friend Peter that he would die but I would remain until he comes again. And he was right. Peter did die. They all died, long ago. All but me.*
>
> *The thread that began on that beach has traveled across the centuries, through many locations, until now. He did not explain why I was left behind and I do not know how much longer I must remain, until he comes to take me home.*
>
> *Over the span of my life, I have met and known many people, as you can imagine. Our Lord calls us to love our neighbors, as a sign*

of our love for him. That means loving even our enemies, as he did when he forgave those who would go so far as to crucify him. Over the centuries of my life, I have struggled at times to love my enemies.

To love others means that we must empty ourselves of the self-love that is so suffocating. It is only when we empty ourselves that the Holy Spirit can enter and fill us with a new love, the very love of Christ. And it is only in his power that we are able to love as he calls us to love.

I believe that I have seen you empty yourself as you stood up to a brutal attack, placing yourself at risk for my sake, to defend an old man like me. And I know that the Spirit of Christ has filled you. Now, you have learned to love, because he first loved you. You have been filled with his love, a love that will never die.

My prayer for you is that you are able to carry this love back to your old life in America, to heal wounds and broken relationships, and to seek out the lost. May the love of Christ flow through you like a rushing fountain.

I will miss you, Millie. Perhaps our paths will cross again, though I think not. But when our Lord comes, riding upon the clouds, and when he releases me from enduring the continuing mystery of this life, look for me. I will be looking for you, Millie.

Blessings, Juan

Millie closed her eyes after finishing the letter, brushed back the tears, and thought how appropriate that he called his life a "thread."

As she grew more alert and mobile, Millie was able to assess the damage to her arm. She learned that the bleeding had been stopped and her arm sewn up by a local doctor in Santiago. But muscles and tendons had been torn and would not heal on their own. She would have no use of her right arm without extensive reconstructive surgery and even then, a long-term rehabilitation program would be required.

Millie was determined to get up and around, to ready herself for the trip home. Frank would accompany her. She knew that Douglas Parks and Dr. Chandler would be anxious for a debrief session with her and

Frank, and she dreaded reporting back to them. They would want to know if she and Frank had found the Apostle John and she would tell them that they had not.

Millie and Frank could have phoned in their report, but she was able to put it off with the thought that her report was too sensitive for a phone call. She didn't want to violate Douglas Parks' security rules!

Millie did phone Randall as soon as she could speak without sounding groggy. She deliberately minimized her injury, reasoning that he would find out how bad it was soon enough anyway. He was understandably anxious and offered to fly to Spain to take her home. Millie assured him, however, that she'd be fine traveling home with Frank.

The day arrived for their departure. It was difficult to thank Enrique enough for his hospitality, his protection and for his mastery of so many moving parts with the entire adventure. She was sensitive to the loss of his cousin Victor Cardenas and knew that he was still grieving that loss. And of course, she was grateful for Miguel, who had literally saved her life. Miguel would drive Millie and Frank to Barcelona for their return flight.

Once back in the States, the first order of business was to debrief with Douglas Parks and Dr. Chandler. They accepted the story, just as Frank had, that Marianne's attack was aimed at Millie and not Juan. And they were relieved to learn that Marianne had been held in custody for trial in Spain. She would not be going anywhere, anytime soon.

However, there was more bad news from Parks. Millie wondered to herself if Douglas Parks ever had any good news, but she kept quiet.

Parks reported that Marianne had done more damage to the software and the database than first thought.

"It appears now that as she was programming on the software, she was able to allow only a few of the matches to be reported to us through the system, enough to keep us from suspecting anything. Other matches, however, bypassed our reports and went straight into a file that found its way outside our protective security, presumably to *La Noche de Oscuridad*.

"We have just now recovered these matches and several of them look promising. We can only hope that the death of Hans Oltorf and the detention of Marianne Weems might slow down their search long enough for us to catch up. We have no idea as to any others from *La Noche* who may be hunting for John."

"Frank," began Dr. Chandler, "would you be willing to follow up on these new candidates? And Millie, once your arm is healed, how about you?"

"I will be happy to continue," Frank responded. "But I don't know if you are aware of the severity of Millie's wounds. However, she can certainly speak for herself."

"I believe," began Millie, "that I should retire from this project. I have visited four locations, resulting in the death of one candidate, Father Cardenas, the attempted assassination of a second, Charles Boutte, and the threat of death feared by the third, Geoffrey Smythe. I never knew if you considered Enrique as a candidate, but it seems that only he is safe. Perhaps I'm bad luck but anyway, I do not believe I am fit to make another trip."

Her omission of any comment about Juan hopefully cemented his absence from their list of candidates.

"Millie, I don't believe it's fair in any way to consider yourself responsible for what happened to any of the candidates whom you visited," answered Parks. "And by the way, we did not consider Enrique as a candidate. We sent you to him at his request, presumably to keep you safe from attack. Unsuccessfully, it would appear."

Dr. Chandler's face showed his disappointment in her decision. "Millie, I am so sorry that it's turned out this way" he said. "But I understand, I really do."

The conversation ended on that note, with no suspicion that she was keeping any secrets.

"Millie, I am so happy to see you," Sister Camilla beamed as Millie sat down in front of her after returning home. Millie had been home only two days before returning to visit with Sister at the Abbey. "Let me hear about your adventures."

Millie recounted her story, careful to avoid using names or revealing secrets. "It has all been so much," she went on, "and it's hard for me to reflect on it without wondering what it has been all about."

"To me," Sister Camilla began, "it sounds as if you have learned and lived a new dimension of love, a deeper love, a love that has been granted to you by our Holy Father. It is a love made possible only through suffering, not only physical wounds, but also emotional pain, such as your grief for the priest in Guatemala. That love, refined through suffering, is the love of our Lord, the love we are invited to share if we are willing to live the life that he offers."

"Yes," responded Millie, "for whatever reason, I feel so much more alive, even though I am more physically hurt than I have ever been."

"Well, my child," concluded the tiny nun, "you seem to be in a different place from when we last spoke. Now that you've opened wide the door to his love, you have joined the dance, his dance, the dance of love. I hope and pray that you never close that door."

After scheduling her surgery, Millie wanted to make a short trip to Plostina. Her surgeon had told Millie that recovery would be slow and painful, but that she would regain much (but not all) of the use of her right arm. So, she wanted to make this mini-pilgrimage to Plostina beforehand. She asked Randall to join her.

While Randall waited at the car, Millie stood in the little cemetery, where her parents and Father Vlacek were buried, under the now-aging oak that he had planted so long ago. Millie brought with her the old wooden box containing the linen handkerchief with the dangling thread.

"Father Vlacek," she began, tears forming in her eyes, "do you remember me? I'm Millie, the little girl who grew up here, and who went to your church. You baptized me, remember? You used to call me your 'dangling thread,' do you remember that? You used to say that there was much more to me than it seemed. For the longest time, I didn't believe you. Actually, I didn't really want to believe you.

"And Father Vlacek, I didn't believe because I thought that my life could never be anything more than a normal life, a predictable life. And so I hid in the familiar, the comfortable, and in what was expected of me, never daring to extend myself into anything new or uncertain.

"But then, my thread was pulled, and pulled hard. It was pulled into uncertainty, and danger and excitement and yes, love. But always, despite the twists and turns, it made a difference that you had believed in me. It truly did.

"And now, I've come back to stand beneath the tree that you planted so long ago. I've come to report back to you, Father. All that I can say is that you were right. You were right, Father Vlacek. I went out from Plostina into the world and tried to hide from it. But life pulled me into a stream that was twisting and turning in a way that I couldn't see. I couldn't see where it was going. I couldn't see anything. But I plunged in anyway.

"And Father Vlacek, that stream turned out to be a stream of love. God's love. It was a stream of great joy and also a stream of pain and suffering, not just for me but for others as well. And yet through the pain and suffering, great love emerged.

"Father, I believe the thread has been pulled all the way now. I'm going to give it away. Yes, Father, I am going to give the box and the linen with the dangling thread to someone else, someone who has great promise but who cannot yet see. It should go to a person who cannot yet see that life, the true life that God wants to give us, can be found only by accepting the invitation to pull the thread.

"I don't yet know who I will give it to, Father. But I have faith that our Lord will show me."

As she returned to the car, Randall retrieved a package from the trunk. "Millie, I almost forgot. This arrived the other day, addressed to you. It was delivered to our house by courier, with no identification of who sent it. I haven't opened it, but perhaps now is a good time for you to do so." And he handed her a postal box, wrapped in packing paper.

"You are going to have to open it for me, Randall," she said. "You're going to have to do many things for me until I have recovered."

"Yes," he responded, "yes, I intend to do just that." And he removed the wrapping paper to reveal a small jewelry box. "I will open it, but remember, this is for you, Millie."

And Randall opened the small box, pulling out the cotton padding on the inside, to reveal a silver scallop on a silver strand. Inside was a hand-written note. It read:

> *Millie, I am so happy that you are now home and safe. I still think of you and I still pray for you. Hopefully you will also remember me with some affection.*
>
> *I know that I explained to you the symbolic meaning of the scallop and why it is used so much on the Camino. But now, I have been given a new meaning for it. You see, the grooves on the scallop go both ways. God's love radiates from a central point outward, just like the grooves, to all who will receive him. And to all of creation, in fact. That love is returned, through the same grooves, back to that central point, to our Holy Father, Son and Spirit. These three are in a relationship of love, one that we can all join.*
>
> *All that we need to join in this love, Millie, is to get in the groove!*
>
> *Millie, I hope that you will accept this token of our time together and I hope that you will wear the scallop to remind you of God's love in your life. Maybe from time to time it might also remind you of our pilgrimage on the Camino.*
>
> *I know, Millie, that you have been on a long journey. A journey that has been hard and painful at times. Perhaps that is what it takes to get in the groove of God's love. Why? Because when we find ourselves on a long and painful journey, we find that our traveling companion on that journey is none other than God himself.*
>
> *And that is what I have found in you, Millie.*
>
> *Blessings, Juan*

Millie read Juan's note and read it again, choking back tears. She silently turned to Randall and as she did, he opened the door of the car.

While Millie carefully entered the front seat, bracing herself with her left arm, Randall slipped the silver scallop around her neck. She kissed him lightly on the cheek. "Let's go home, Randall, and begin again."

ABOUT THE AUTHOR

Robert Westheimer is the author of *When God Calls, How Do You Answer?* and *Dangling.* He is a member of the Chapelwood United Methodist Church in Houston, Texas.

Westheimer studied at the University of Texas and spent his career as a certified public accountant and partner of Arthur Andersen & Co. He is married with two children and four grandchildren.